FROM DA BIG ISLAND

NEW YORK DEFINED HER
HAWAII CHANGED HER

BILL HUTCHINSON

Published by Bill Hutchinson
Web Site: http://FromDaBigIsland.com
Facebook: https://www.facebook.com/FromDaBigIsland
Twitter: @FromDaBigIsland

Paperback ISBN-13: 978-0-9996268-0-1
Hardback ISBN-13: 978-0-9996268-1-8
eBook ISBN-13: 978-0-9996268-2-5
Large print ISBN-13: 978-0-9996268-3-2

10 9 8 7 6 5 4 3

Dedication

This book is dedicated to my beloved husband Allyn for all his help, inspiration, and creativity over the years.

BILL HUTCHINSON

Characters

Auntie: Ruth's uphill neighbor and horticulturist.

Ben Kokua: Ruth's live-in handyman and gardener.

Danny Mauka: Hawaii television producer and station manager.

Eileen Baccio: Wife of Joe Baccio.

George Epstein: Zach Newcomb's law partner.

Gloria La Fong: Ruth's therapist.

Jim: Network CEO.

Joe Baccio: Head of a New York crime syndicate and client of Law Offices of Newcomb and Epstein.

Linda: Ruth's sister and mother of Pauline.

Meka Ayala: Ruth's downhill neighbor, husband of Nalai, and William's father.

Michael Kokua: Ben's musician brother.

Mrs. Charlene Strong: Honokaa High School counselor.

Mrs. Wiggins: Ruth's cat.

Nalani Ayala: Ruth's downhill neighbor, wife of Meka, and William's mother.

Paul Martin: Sarah's husband and owner of a house in Hawaii.

Pauline: Ruth's niece and a television production assistant.

Ruth Newcomb: The protagonist, Zack's wife and star of the syndicated television show *From the Big Apple*.

Sarah Martin: Ruth's childhood friend, Paul's wife, *From the Big Apple* television show producer, and owner of a house in Hawaii.

William Ayala: Son of Meka and Nalani, Ruth's downhill neighbors, and an at risk high school student who would rather surf than be in class.

Zach Newcomb: Ruth's husband and George Epstein's law partner.

BILL HUTCHINSON

Table of Contents

PROLOGUE

Ruth Newcomb and I go back a good many years; more years than either would like to admit. She is very staid in her ways, sticking more to the familiar than the unfamiliar. Even though she had been on the Big Island of Hawaii for what would seem decades, it has only been a little more than one.

Ruth is part of my ohana. Ohana is Hawaiian for what most would call extended family. Every time I return to the Big Island, we get together, sitting for hours on her lanai (Hawaiian for veranda or porch), talk about life, old stories from before we met, bringing each other up to date with our lives, and other things friends enjoy discussing.

On one particular trip, we were seated on Ruth's lanai talking, just as we have always done. What made this time different, more than any other, was Ruth's recollection of when we first met and events surrounding her arrival on the Big Island. Not that I was contesting it, nor anything like that, she wanted to validate her own memory. Period!

Ruth told me to remain seated, got up, and went to her small living room library to get a journal; one of the many volumes that she had written since reading *The Diary of*

Anne Frank. Little did Ruth realize at that time, her first diary would become numerous volumes, filling the lower shelves of her library. Seeing her return with one of the journals in hand, that's when it struck me, I'm a journalist, why not write a book about Ruth's transition from the Big Apple to the Big Island of Hawaii, using her journals as a basis for turning them into this book you are now reading.

William Ayala
Huntington Beach, CA
September 11, 2017

RUTH

"Ruth, Ruth Newcomb, is that you?" an elderly woman yelled, running after Ruth, a red-haired lady, who continued her brisk walk down New York's post 9/11 Fifth Avenue totally oblivious of the Christmas shoppers and the woman calling her name. It wasn't hard to miss Ruth, as not many people have red-hair to begin with, and most of the other women wore scarves or hats to protect their heads from the wind. However, to Ruth, it is her red hair and staunch demeanor, that anyone who would see her, will instantly recognize her as television personality Ruth Newcomb. If that were not enough, Ruth was always impeccably dressed and wore the latest designer fashion. Her clothes were always skintight to show off her slender well-proportioned body, fitting her like a glove, not bad for a lady in her sixties. So it was no surprise that the old woman had instantly recognized Ruth Newcomb.

The elderly woman finally reached Ruth and tapped her on the shoulder, "Aren't you Ruth Newcomb; *From the Big Apple?*"

Ruth stopped and turned, "Of course, Darling! Who else could I be?"

The elderly woman dug through her purse, "I'm such a big fan of your show." This was a stall technique Ruth had heard many times before as fans searched for a pad and pen. Finding both, the woman held them in front of Ruth and asked, "May I have your autograph?"

Happy to oblige a fan, Ruth took the pen and pad, and scribbled something and signed the pad, handed both back to the old woman who studied it. The autograph was not the normal, everyday one would expect from famous people, the signature was unique, and one that was instantly recognizable to her vast television audience. She would sign her name Ruth Newcomb surrounding her signature with the large stylized apple associated her show, *From the Big Apple*. The woman looked back at Ruth smiling, "Oh, thank you. Thank you. It's such a wonderful and unusual autograph, one that I will cherish for years to come."

"Thank you, Darling." Ruth responded. She always used darling when responding to people as it was a general response people expected and liked, and perhaps most of all, she liked using darling because it was easier than remembering the person's name. Ruth turned to continue her walk through the Fifth Avenue Christmas crowd as a light evening snow begun to fall. As she reached 52nd Street, the crossing light hand popped up. She stopped with the hordes of people. The aroma of cooking steaks caused Ruth to look to her right, where she spotted the steel jockeys lining the front of The 21 Club.

A man accidentally bumped into Ruth and in a thick Italian accent said, "Excusa me." For some reason, perhaps the combination of seeing The 21 Club and the Italian accent caused Ruth to flashback to that one unusual evening, many years ago, when Mario Manzoni, the head of one of New York's key crime families, was assassinated in front of the restaurant.

It was the evening of June 17th, 1965. A warm pleasant breeze blew down 52nd Street past The 21 Club. A large crowd of spectators surrounded the red carpet and the chrome stanchions holding the rope leading from the entrance to the street to the two awaiting stretch limousines. A television news crew was set up at the entrance of the club. Bob, the cameraman, had his camera on Pat, the local New York television commentator, standing next to one of limousines. Looking at the camera, speaking into his microphone, Pat announced, "This is Pat Patterson at The 21 Club, where in a few moments mob boss Mario Manzoni, his lieutenant Joe Baccio, attorney Zach Newcomb, along with their wives will be exiting. It is rumored they have been discussing a resolution to the turf wars between the Manzoni and the Sarducci crime families."

In the nighttime crowd next to Pat, stood a tall black haired man who wore an unbuttoned long black raincoat, which would be more suited for winter than a warm June evening. No one seemed to notice the man was concealing a gun under his raincoat.

"Manzoni," continued Pat, "prefers the use of the legal system to resolve conflict over the use of force as some of the other crime families do."

The doorman opened the door for two bodyguards, in their early 20's dressed in black, with slicked back black hair. Pat noticed the two bodyguards leaving and changed his commentary, "it looks like they are exiting the 21 Club."

The bodyguards made their way to the limousines, scanning the crowd, not noticing the man in the long heavy raincoat. The doorman opened the door, this time for gray haired Mario Manzoni, who wore a white tuxedo, and his blond bombshell of a wife, some twenty years younger, wore a white sequenced Dior evening dress. They were followed by Joe Baccio, dressed in a white tuxedo, and Eileen, his wife, dressed a vivid blue evening gown.

"Here comes Mario Manzoni and Joe Baccio along with their wives."

They were followed by Ruth, dressed in a brilliant shimmering green evening dress, and Zach, her husband, in a white tuxedo.

"Here's Zach Newcomb and his wife, Ruth Newcomb, our very own junior reporter."

As Ruth left the club, she saw Pat and mouthed, "I love you, darling." and threw him a kiss.

Mario, not one to miss an opportunity for publicity, waved and approached Pat.

"Mario, do you have anything you are willing to tell us?" Pat asked. The assassin in the raincoat stealthy pulled out the gun and shot Mario at point-blank range.

Mario fell to the ground, his wife screamed and grabbed him, as blood gushed out covering his white tuxedo and splattered both his wife and Pat with blood. The assassin turned, bumping Pat, at the same instant one of the bodyguards fired his gun, hitting Pat, who collapsed next to Mario and his wife.

Meanwhile, the surrounding crowd dropped to the ground in an attempt to avoid being caught in the crossfire. The bodyguards started to chase the running assassin. More gun shots rang out. This time, the assassin fell dead on the sidewalk.

Ruth and Zach, being in the middle of the assassination, surveyed the carnage.

"I think we're safe now that the assassin is dead." Zach assured Ruth. "We need to wait for the police."

"Pat's dead!" Ruth exclaimed, shaking her head in disbelief. "I need to get this news story to the newsroom, now!" She noticed Bob had captured the entire bloodbath and was filming the blood covered body of Mario being held by his wife, much like the Pieta, with Pat lying to the side in a pool of blood.

"Bob, darling, when you have an opportunity, don't forget to get an wide shot for the closing showing restaurant with the jockeys." Ruth commanded. She looked at Pat and spotted the blood covered microphone. Trembling, she bent down, using her thumb and forefinger, picked the microphone up by the wire mesh which didn't have blood and wiped Pat's blood off on his blue news jacket. As Ruth regained her composure, she pointed the microphone down, and in a strong whisper said, "Bob! Bob, darling! Turn the camera on me. I'll finish the piece. Then get the footage back to the studio. We need to make the eleven o'clock news!"

Bob turned the camera around towards Ruth, and gave her the queue. Taking a deep breath, Ruth brought the microphone up looking into the camera, "This is Ruth Newcomb, reporting to you from The 21 Club, where a few moments ago we witnessed the brutal murder of Mario Manzoni, the reputed mob boss, and television commentator, Pat Patterson, by a lone assassin ..."

"Andiamo, we go, light change!" Ruth was knocked back into the present day as the light at 52nd Street changed and the man with the Italian accent pushed his way past her. Ruth continued her short walk down Fifth Avenue finally reaching Rockefeller Center. When she entered the plaza, she was greeted by the illuminated Rockefeller Center Christmas tree, the piped in Christmas music playing, skaters enjoying the rink, and the smell of chestnuts roasting wafting from a nearby vending cart. Ruth smiled, nodded her head in approval, and thought to herself, it was indeed Christmastime in New York City.

* * *

Inside the Rockefeller Center television studio, cables, flats, propping, cameras, and personnel were watching the broadcast unfold. Ruth, wore a glimmering silken red dress, seated at the desk on the *From the Big Apple* set. Behind her was a large red stylized apple, just like the one she used in her autograph, with red lettering announcing the show, *From the Big Apple*. The monitor next to the camera was pointed towards Ruth playing a prerecorded segment of the Rockettes Christmas Spectacular. A floor manager stood next to the camera holding one hand up flashing five seconds to go. The countdown continued as he yelled, "4, 3, 2." The signal was given, Ruth looking at the camera, and read from the Teleprompter, "So don't miss the Rockettes Christmas Spectacular at Radio City Music Hall through January second.

"Darlings, you know how I adore the New York Public Library Reading is Fundamental program. I love it so much so, that I will be reading Charles Dickens, *A Christmas Carol* at the New York Public Library mid-town branch this Saturday at two PM. So don't forget to be there because reading is fun-da-mental.

"This wraps up another edition of *From the Big Apple*. Tomorrow we will have..." pausing, she tilted her head, as she gave an inquisitive look at the Teleprompter which read, "TOMORROW WE WILL HAVE ???? UNTIL NEXT TIME..."

Realizing that the question marks were for her to fill in, Ruth quickly recouped, "... a wonderful show for you.

"Until next time, this is Ruth Newcomb, *From the Big Apple*." Ruth looked directly at the camera smiling. The tally light went out.

"We're clear," yelled the floor manager.

Ruth's smile faded as she looked into the camera, "What the heck was that?"

"What was what?" The floor manager responded.

"Darling," addressing the floor manager, "you and Sarah know what I mean."

The floor manager shrugged and gave Ruth an inquisitive look as she continued, "I mean the question marks!"

Sarah Martin, the show's producer and Ruth's childhood friend, ran up.

"I thought we had the next show planned." Ruth asked Sarah.

"We don't!" Ruth's niece Pauline, a twenty-something production assistant who wants to be a producer, was carrying a clipboard following Sarah like a puppy, was the first to speak.

"Pauline, darling, would you be a doll and get auntie some water?"

As Pauline left, Ruth looked at the television monitor next to the camera, which was showing a commercial with palm trees, sandy beaches, Diamond Head, and Waikiki Beach.

"In any event," Sarah continued, "George called during the segment and canceled."

"So what if he canceled, Sarah. You could have had Teleprompter Bob put something other than those darn question marks. Darling, you know how I hate that."

"You did a good job faking it."

Ruth returned her gaze to the monitor when the commercial ended with *Come to Hawaii.*

"Sarah, I could have said, 'Tomorrow we will be coming to you from Hawaii!'"

"Coming to you from Hawaii?"

Ruth raised her voice, "yes, Hawaii! Ever since Thanksgiving, that *Come to Hawaii* ad has aired. We might as well do the show from Hawaii. What's going on here?"

Sarah, tried not to be defensive, "It's cold; people want to get away to a warm climate like Hawaii. You know, warm friendly happy people, tropical drinks, ukuleles, luaus, hukilaus, and Hula dancing."

"Not everyone has a little grass shack in Hawaii like you and Paul do. Some people like to ski; go to a cozy cabin in the mountains, and enjoy the snow."

"And then there are those like you who never step foot out of New York."

Pauline returned with Ruth's water. "Thank you, Darling."

Sarah looked at Ruth, "we need to think of something for the next show."

"Maybe we could do *The Nutcracker.*"

Both Sarah and Pauline grimaced and in unison declared, "Not again!"

Pauline continued, "We've never done an inside tour of Tiffany's which we can tie into the rerelease of *Breakfast at Tiffany's.* Or maybe we can cover the medicinal marijuana trial Uncle Zach is working on. Sparks are flying and I'm sure we can do an interview with Uncle Zach about why the Baccio trail is so important."

Across the room, a production assistant yelled, "Pauline, telephone." Pauline turned and walked quickly to the phone.

Sarah agreeing with Pauline's line of thinking responded, "We did *The Nutcracker* last year. Think of something. We'll talk about it at the production meeting."

"Darling, I was thinking of an easy way out."

"I'm with you." Sarah put her hand on Ruth's shoulder, "We're still on for Charlie Chan tonight, aren't we?"

"Starts at seven." Ruth responded. Sarah removed her arm and turned to leave. Ruth continued, "I have the chopsticks ready, so don't forget the sushi."

"Big Apple or Mr. Okomoto Sushi?"

NUMBER 3 BEEKMAN PLACE

Ruth's movie room resembled a 1930's style theater with red curtains flanking a large projection screen. Zach, Ruth's husband, and Paul, Sarah's husband, were seated together in an overstuffed leather love seat eating popcorn. Next to them in another love seat were Ruth and Sarah. Mrs. Wiggins, Ruth's portly elderly black cat given to her years ago and named by Carol Burnett, was curled up on Ruth's lap. In front of them are empty Mr. Okomoto Sushi containers and freshly prepared Manhattans.

"Manhattan's, sushi, popcorn, and Charlie Chan... cheers!" Zach said as they all toasted. He reached for the remote and pressed the button. On the screen, *Charlie Chan and the Black Camel* started, the credits rolled by, followed by a scene of surfers surfing in the foreground and Diamond Head in the background. A few moments later was a shot of 1930's Waikiki Beach from the surfer's point of view with the only two multistory hotels; the Royal Hawaiian and the Halekulani.

Paul whispered to Zach, "that reminds me..."

"Shhh..." Sarah said quietly.

Paul ignored Sarah and continued only in a lower voice, "that reminds me, Charlie liked to have his Manhattan's at the Halekulani House Without a Key Bar under the kiawe tree."

"House Without a Key? Kiawe tree?" Zach responded.

Ruth and Sarah gave the guys disapproving looks. Ruth unable to concentrate on the movie and asked, "Can't you guys let us enjoy the movie?"

Zach grabbed the remote, pausing the movie.

"What are you doing?" Ruth protested.

"Paul was saying something about Charlie and the Hall-le-ku-lani House Without a Key Bar ..."

"Oh, that!" Sarah retorts. "It's nothing. The real Charlie Chan hung out at the Halekulani Hotel and its House Without a Key Bar, it is as simple as that."

"Honey, I thought you like your tropical drinks and listening to the live Hawaiian music under the kiawe tree at sunset." Paul exclaimed.

"I do, darling, it's a fantastic hotel, but we're here to watch a movie, not talk about Hawaii." Sarah responded.

Zach pressed the button on the remote and the movie continued. The girls were content and smiled.

"Thanks!" The girls respond in unison.

Neither Zach nor Paul are interested in the movie. Their eyes wonder around the room. Zach starts whispering to Paul again, "I thought you liked the remoteness of your vacation home on the Big Island."

"We do, eccentric neighbors and all; something straight out of a Ma and Pa Kettle movie or *The Beverly Hillbillies*."

Ruth glared at the two of them, grabbed the remote, pressed the pause button, and asked, "So you want to watch Ma and Pa Kettle?"

"No, we're talking about our house on the Big Island of Hawaii," Paul responded.

"Darling," Sarah addressing Paul, "they already told us they don't want to go to Hawaii. Why push it?" Sarah then looked at Zach, "Zach always has an excuse of being tied up on this or that trial. And..." Sarah looked at Ruth, "Ruth doesn't want to leave the comfort of the Big Apple." Sarah looked at the screen. "Now that we have everything cleared up, let's watch the movie." Ruth pressed the play button and everyone turned their attention towards the screen and resumed watching Charlie Chan.

* * *

Auntie Mame was always Ruth's favorite novel, so much so, she vowed when she grew up, she would live in the very place Auntie Mame lived, Number 3 Beekman Place. It took years for Ruth and Zach to obtain the apartment with the terrace overlooking the East River on the secluded two block long residential street, just north of the United Nations building.

The Christmas decorations filled the penthouse sunroom as the light from the rising sun over the East River cast a golden glow across the room. Mrs. Wiggins was playing with one of the Christmas ornament balls hanging nearby.

Dressed in woolen robes, Ruth and Zach were seated at the table drinking coffee and having breakfast. Ruth took a sip of coffee from her Tiffany coffee cup and glanced at Zach finishing his half eaten bagel reading the *New York Times*. Ruth noticed the headline *Defense Atty Newcomb Drops Bombshell at Baccio Trial*. "What's this about a bombshell?"

"A bombshell?" Zach exclaimed. "It's only the beginning! The medicinal marijuana issue came to a head yesterday."

"Darling, you know marijuana is bad. I don't understand why you are for it."

"I'm not. Joe thinks since states have started to allow medicinal marijuana, it's another way to make money."

"Darling, I don't understand it at all. People are using the medicinal excuse to get high."

"We have documentation that it does help some people."

Ruth, having finished her breakfast, got up. "Got to run." She went over and kissed Zach, who smiled as she left the terrace.

THE NUTCRACKER

The studio office corridor was filled with business people dressed in holiday colors scurrying about. Pauline stood by the elevator, repeatedly looked at her watch and took an occasional sip from her coconut water while she waited for Ruth. Ding, the elevator door opened, people exited, while others entered, the door closed. Another look at the watch followed by a sip. Ding, the elevator door opened, people exited, door closed. Ding, the third elevator door opened. This time, Ruth, dressed her woolen coat and scarf, stepped out of the elevator.

"Aunt Ruth, great show yesterday. Nothing like the Rockettes!"

Ruth nodded, "You said it, Pauline."

Ruth strode towards her office. Pauline ran to keep up.

"So we're doing another segment on *The Nutcracker*?"

"Haven't decided yet."

"When are you and Uncle Zach seeing it?"

"Tomorrow."

Sarah caught up with Ruth and Pauline. "Good news! I was able to get Alec Baldwin for today's show."

"Great!" Ruth and Pauline respond in unison.

Ruth noticed Pauline taking a sip from her coconut water. "Pauline, why are you drinking that stuff?"

"Coconut water is a great alternative to other drinks as it is all-natural, healthy and potassium rich among other things. Some call it 'Mother Nature's sports drink.'"

"Sounds like you're an advertisement." Ruth responded as they entered her office. Ruth hung her coat and scarf on the coat stand. The office was clean with a special feminine air about it. Flowers on the desk, plant in the corner, goldfish bowl on the credenza next to an Emmy, and needlepoint "I Love New York" pillow on the plush leather sofa. On the wall was a framed "Reading Is Fun" poster from the New York Metropolitan Library with Ruth holding *The Adventures of Huckleberry Finn* in the center. Pictures of Ruth with the Clintons, Donald Trump, Jackie Onassis, Princess Dianna and Prince Charles adorn the walls along with diplomas from New York and Columbia Universities and a plaque for the Nobel Prize in Journalism. Behind her desk was a spectacular view of the New York skyline. Ruth sat at the desk, placed her purse in the top right drawer. Sarah and Pauline took seats across from Ruth's desk.

"We need to work on the show," Sarah stated. "We cannot do another year of *The Nutcracker.*"

"Darling," Ruth responded, "I was trying to make things easy and we're seeing it tomorrow night."

"We will need a different angle than what we've done in the past. Any suggestions?"

"I see, making me do all the work! Hmm…"

"We might as well run last year's show."

Ruth laughed. "You're so funny, Sarah. How about the fight scene between the soldiers and the mice or the costumes and make-up?"

Sarah started taking notes. "That's a thought."

"Sure, the conflict, the intrigue, the combat. Finally, the soldiers all dead …" Ruth said jokingly, "Not unlike living in New York." They all laughed.

"It is Christmas!" Sarah exclaimed, "and fights don't mix, Ruth. The Sugar Plum Fairy and the Nutcracker dance sequence is more Christmassy."

"Do we always have to sugar coat it?" Ruth asked.

They all laughed again.

"You know what I'm talking about. You're the one who mentioned *The Nutcracker*."

"I was trying to keep things simple," Ruth admitted.

Pauline glanced at the framed New York Metropolitan Library *Reading is Fun* poster. "Aunt Ruth, you always do a great job at reading *A Christmas Carol*. Maybe we could do a segment on that instead of *The Nutcracker*."

"That's an idea," Sarah exclaimed. "Let's keep our options open. Best of all, we have Alec this afternoon and are going to see *The Nutcracker* tomorrow."

* * *

The following evening, Ruth and Zach were in their master bathroom vanity area getting dressed in formal attire. Zach was unsuccessfully attempting to put on his black onyx cuff links. Ruth noticed he was having difficulty and helped Zach put them on. She reached into her jewelry case and took out her triple-strand pearl necklace. Without saying a word, Zach lovingly took the necklace from her and started to put it on Ruth's neck. As he does so, she turned her back to him, to make it easier for Zach to attach the necklace. After fastening the clasp, he stood back, giving Ruth an affectionate whack on her derrière. "You're so beautiful! And these pearls make you look fantastic!" Ruth smiled as Zach turned her around for a long hug and affectionate kiss.

* * *

At Lincoln Center, a light snow was falling, adding to the magic of the evening performance of *The Nutcracker*. Limousines pulled up alongside taxis and cars. Exiting from one limousine were Ruth, Zach, Sarah, and Paul, all dressed in formal attire. The foursome walked with the other theater goers as the falling snow glistened reflecting the lights illuminating the fountain. Large posters announce *The Nutcracker* as they made their way towards the golden lit Lincoln Center entrance.

During the performance, Ruth and Sarah looked at each other smiling as the Nutcracker and the mice began to battle. Sarah noticed Ruth had reached into her purse and pulled out a notepad, and whispered, "Enjoy it! You don't need to take notes."

"Darling, you know me, I need to."

Sarah placed her hand on the notepad and shook her head. Ruth started to pay attention to the ballet.

❋ ❋ ❋

The mezzanine was filled with people dressed in black tie and Christmas colored evening gowns, sipping Champagne or wine. Ruth, Zach, Sarah, and Paul were sequestered in a corner sipping Champagne. Ruth enthusiastically exclaimed, "The fight sequence was better than past years. However, I don't think we have enough to do a full eight minute segment on this version being any different."

Paul smiled retorting, "Wait until the third act."

"During the Sugar Plum Fairy and the Nutcracker dance." Zach added.

Paul leaned into the girls, "We heard rumor that they are seeing each other."

"Who's seeing whom?" Sarah inquired.

"The Sugar Plum Fairy and the Nutcracker, who else?" Zach answered.

"Oh, stop it, you two." Ruth exclaimed.

"We're not kidding. In real life Rudolph and Natasha are seeing each other. I heard that scene makes the show." Paul responded.

Zach noticed Joe and Eileen Baccio, now in their sixties, walking up to the foursome. "Joe, I didn't know you were going to be here tonight." Zach said as he extended his hand to Joe. "You enjoying the show?"

"Fantastic!" Joe responded. "The tension between the Sugar Plum Fairy and the Nutcracker is unbelievable! I don't recall that from prior performances."

"Zach put you up to this didn't he, Joe?" Sarah asked.

"Up to what?"

"Oh, never mind." Sarah shaking her head, continued. "How's the trial going?"

Millie, a woman in her fifties carrying a *Playbill* program and pen, made her way to the group, followed by her meek short portly balding husband in tow, interrupted the conversation. "You're Ruth Newcomb of *From the Big Apple*, aren't you?"

"Darling, who else could I be?"

"I *adore* your show. May I have your autograph?" Millie pushed the *Playbill* program and the pen towards Ruth.

"Darling, what's your name?"

"Millie ... Millie Greenwald."

Ruth looked at Millie's husband, who looked down, avoiding eye contact with Ruth and the others in her party.

"Do you want me to add your husband's name, too?"

Millie smiled, clasped her hands together, looked up at Ruth. "Oh, could you? Please! His name is Billy." The husband smiled.

"Ah, Millie and Billy, what a pair!" Ruth laughed followed by everyone else, as she signed the front of the *Playbill* program. "To Millie and Billy, My favorite fans, Ruth Newcomb." She drew her stylized *From the Big Apple* logo around her signature. Ruth handed the program back to Millie. Both Millie and Billy looked at the signature on the *Playbill* program smiling as they received the best Christmas gift ever.

"Oh, thank you so much, Mrs. Newcomb. Thank you and Merry Christmas."

Millie and Billy both bowed as if they were in the presence of royalty, turning, they left the group.

"Ruth, every time we get together your fans interrupt. Don't you ever get tired of it?" Eileen asked.

"Not in the least, Eileen." Ruth answered, "It's expected. Now, where were we?"

"Sarah was asking how things were going with the trial." Joe responded. "I think it's going better than expected. We're dealing with medicinal marijuana; it in itself is enough to cause major issues."

The first chime rang. The audience started to head into the theater. A few looked at Ruth and smiled, giving her a nod, as they passed the group. Ruth nodded back.

"I believe the medicinal marijuana is the way to go," Joe continued. "Legalize it, not only here, but nationwide, and tax it. The government makes money, I make money, and everyone will be happy." The second chime is heard. "We better get back to our seats. Hope you all have a wonderful evening. See you later. Merry Christmas!" Joe and Eileen turn and join the theater going crowd as they return to their seats.

* * *

As the audience exited Lincoln Center, they were greeted by a heavy snow, which had already blanketed the plaza. Ruth, Zach, Sarah, and Paul made their way through one of the shoveled paths to the awaiting limousines at street level. After a few moments, their limousine pulled up. Inside, they brushed the snow from their jackets, as the limousine headed down Broadway towards Columbus Circle. Ruth starts the conversation, "Let's focus on the Rudolf and Natasha romance."

"We can't," Sarah responded.

"Why not, Darling? I think that's what made the show so good."

"We need to verify if the romance is true or not."

"Pshaw!" Ruth responded as the limousine entered Columbus Circle with the other cars, trucks, taxis, and limousines whizzing unencumbered through the snow, ice, and slush. Over Sarah's shoulder, through the limousine window, Ruth watched in horror as a large truck skidding sideways was headed directly towards the side of the limousine where Sarah was seated. Ruth stiffened and yelled, "Brace yourselves!"

POST MORTEM

Ruth was in a hospital bed, eyes closed. Bottles filled with Ringer's and other solutions hung from hooks attached to a bar attached to the bed. All the tubes connected to her arm. Ruth opened her eyes, blinking, and scanned the room. The counter was completely covered with flowers and cards; larger flower arrangements had condolences ribbons on them. On the floor next to the counter was a large *From the Big Apple* logo flower arrangement with black and white carnations on its own stand with a ribbon stating "Our thoughts are with you."

Pauline and Linda, Pauline's mother and Ruth's look-alike albeit blonde sister, entered the room carrying a large bouquet of flowers.

"Everyone sends their condolences. I never knew black flowers were so hard to come by." Pauline declared as she moved one of the flower arrangements on the counter to make room for her display.

"Darling, you look much better than we expected considering what you've been through," Linda remarked. "We are all surprised that anyone survived that nasty crash."

"It's been on every news channel." Pauline added.

"What are you talking about?" inquired Ruth.

"The accident," Sarah added, "you were the sole survivor. The impact of the truck was so hard, it trapped everyone inside. The fire department was able to get you out before the limo exploded in flames killing everyone else. You're so lucky!"

* * *

A persistent rain fell at the Brooklyn cemetery filled with cars, limousines, news trucks, and large canopies protecting the crowd of mourners surrounding the Newcomb headstone. Ruth was prominently seated front row center flanked by Linda and Pauline, consoling her. Next to Pauline sat Madam Gloria La Fong, Ruth's born-again hippy therapist, who wore a black Indian tunic. Next to Linda were Joe and Eileen Baccio, along with George Epstein, Zach's law partner and executor of the estate.

The funeral was hard on Ruth. During the ceremony, she was in a daze, which was quite understandable considering what she had gone through and losing those dearest to her. She knew the clock could not be turned back and nothing would be the same as it once was; knowing the deaths would cause a major void in her life, generating unwanted, and unneeded changes. Ruth distained change and wished things would be like they were before the accident.

* * *

Back at Number 3 Beekman Place, in the walk-in closet, Ruth stood in her designer woolen bathrobe, holding Zach's bathrobe, bringing it up to her, taking long smell, remembering intimate moments with Zach. She shook her head, sighed, pensively replaced his robe on its hook.

Ruth meandered into the living room and looked around. A comforting fire in the fireplace added to the melancholy warmth of the room. On the mantel, pictures of Ruth holding an Emmy with Zach and the Martin's at her side, along with photographs of Ruth and Zach having dinner with Jackie Onassis and John F. Kennedy, Jr. at Tavern on the Green, and Ruth and Zach with Donald Trump and Bill and Hillary Clinton all in golf attire. Ruth walked to the Emmy photograph and picked it up. She took it with her to a plush chair next the fireplace. Studying the photograph for a moment, she gently stoked it and smiled. A purring Mrs. Wiggins nudged her leg, letting out a single curt meow. Ruth put the photograph on the side table reached down and stroked the black cat who took the stroking as an invite and leapt up on Ruth's lap, nudging her little black head against Ruth's arm purring. "You're the only one I have left. What are we going to do?"

A cold wind blew down Fifth Avenue as the post-holiday crowd hurried about. Ruth was bundled up in her designer long black woolen coat and red woolen scarf that obscured most of her face. However, she stood out not only wearing her designer outfit, but due to her walking significantly slower than others, moving at a snail's pace. A few people recognized Ruth, smiling and nodding to her. Wanting to avoid the attention, Ruth decided she could walk through Central Park visiting one of her favorite spots, the *Alice in Wonderland* statue which she had not visited in years. She was right; the paths were less crowded except for an occasional squirrel. As she meandered closer to the statue, Ruth heard the sounds of a ukulele and a man singing *My Little Grass Shack*. Curious, Ruth followed the music to the statue where she saw Michael, a Hawaiian Man who wore Ray Bans and an Aloha shirt over his parka. She stopped and listened to the music.

As the song ended, Ruth reached into her purse took out a twenty dollar bill and gently placed it into the open ukulele case which had a few dollar bills and coins.

"Ma-ha-lo!" Michael responded delighted to see the twenty dollars. "Dat mean thank you in Hawaiian."

Ruth started to walk away.

"Aaa-loooo-haa!" Michael said, she paused, looked over her shoulder at him. "Dat mean hello and farewell. Da boss goin do plenny good stuff fo you."

Michael smiled and winked, continuing, "Change, she come soon." before playing the ukulele again.

"I'm just a little Hawaiian,

A homesick island boy,

I want to go back to my fish and poi,

I want to go back to my little grass shack."

Rain prevented Ruth from having dinner on the patio at Central Park's Tavern on the Green. She sat inside, seated solo at a table for two. A solitary candle illuminated her melancholy face. The remains of her half-eaten dinner lay in front of her. She slowly stirred her coffee.

The maître de escorted a middle aged couple to their table, as they passed Ruth's table, the woman recognized Ruth and nudged her husband, who also recognized Ruth. They stopped at her table. The maître de continued walking, unaware that the couple had stopped following him. Ruth was engrossed in her melancholy and continued to stir her coffee, oblivious to anything and everyone around her.

"It must be a terrible loss," the woman interrupted.

Ruth stopped stirring, but did not look up. "Terrible," the woman's husband added, shaking his head, "we miss your show."

Ruth looked up forcing a small, but noticeable smile. The maître de returned to retrieve the couple. "Please follow me."

Ruth took a sip from her coffee. The couple followed the maître de.

Later, the maître de returned to her table. "I'm sorry, Mrs. Newcomb, I should have kept them on a tighter leash."

"Darling, sometimes it cannot be avoided. You did your best under the circumstances."

MORE TIME, PLEASE

The winter was relentless, cold and wetter than previous ones. A cold spring wind blew through the overcast city. Ruth wore her long woolen coat and scarf, standing in front of the modern Upper East Side marble façade of Zach's office building and gazed pensively at the lavishly embossed *Law Offices of Newcomb and Epstein* shiny brass sign. Reaching up with her forefinger, Ruth solemnly traced the outline of her last name. Although the tracing of the word Newcomb took less than a minute, to Ruth it seemed like an eternity. Sighing, she left the sign for the entrance.

"Good morning, Mrs. Newcomb," the legal assistant said. "Is there anything I get you, water perhaps, before you see George?"

"No, darling, I'm fine. Is George ready?"

"Yes, go right in."

A stack of legal papers almost obstructs Ruth's view of George seated behind the desk. The short stocky well-dressed, balding man had on his reading glasses. As Ruth entered, George stood up and motioned to her to take the seat opposite him, smiling he asked, "You like Hawaii?"

"George, you know I've never been."

"Now's your chance."

"Darling, what do you mean?"

"You now own the Martin's house in Honokaa on the Big Island of Hawaii."

Ruth's was flabbergasted.

George continued, "What's also great is the Martins had entered into a ten year contract with the caretaker, Ben Kokua, who lives on the property, and he takes care of the six acres including the macadamia nut orchard."

Ruth shook her head in disbelief.

"It's the perfect vacation home; you don't have to worry about anything."

"If everything has been taken care of, why didn't they give it to ... what's his name?"

"Ben," George paused for a brief moment, "Ben has a heart of gold, is a great caretaker, and is, how should I put it, a little inept."

"Darling, what would I do with a place in Hawaii?"

"At the funeral you told me you wanted to get away from it all, right?"

Ruth nodded.

"What better place than Hawaii?"

"It's so far away."

"You're right, that's what makes it perfect for a vacation home."

"I don't want it."

"It's prime real estate, in a rain forest, with a great view."

"Then make arrangements to sell it."

* * *

Ruth and Jim, the network CEO, entered her office as she went to her desk. "Darling, I need more time," as she sat.

Jim standing in front of the desk, "Ruth, I understand you need more time."

"Jim, darling, I don't think I can continue with the show."

"You've been through a lot, Ruth, and you need to move on. We can't continue the re-runs."

"The show can go on an extended hiatus."

"You realize you are putting a lot of people out of work."

"Stop it, Jim. You're the owner of this network. You will find something to fill the gap until I am ready and you need to fill Sarah's producer position. So let's stop playing games, I'm not into it right now."

"You know me all too well. For you, Ruth, I will reluctantly agree to put the show on hiatus keeping a small contingent of staff to research show ideas for when you return and we will keep this office for you to use. When you're ready to restart *From the Big Apple*, let me know and I'll get the ball rolling."

MADAM LA FONG

Madam Gloria La Fong, Ruth's Earth Mother therapist, wore a long tie-died dress with a Native American Indian turquoise and silver squash blossom necklace, looking much like a born-again hippy, was seated in an overstuffed multicolored bean bag chair with notepad and pen at the ready. The gentle sound of water rippling from a relaxation fountain along with the pleasant tranquil aroma from aromatherapy candles were barely noticeable. The walls were adorned with vintage 1960's Joplin, Elvis, Woodstock, and other posters and memorabilia. Ruth was comfortably seated on one of the numerous bright colored bean bag chairs encircling Madam La Fong.

"I hate it here. I hate my job. I hate it that people stare at me. Everywhere I look, I remember things Zach, Sarah, Paul, and I did. I can't get any of this out of my mind."

"You and Zach were together for going on forty years." Madam La Fong put down her note pad, thinking for a moment. "What happened to you is monumental, there's been a big change in your life; your world has been turned upside down. You not only lost Zach, you lost Sarah, your childhood friend as well."

"Gloria, that's why I'm here. I'm looking to you for guidance."

"It takes people years to get over similar circumstances. Your entire life is changing; you are at the crossroads of life with many paths to take. Over the years you've been given crumbs to help you find your way through changes such as this and when you reach the crossroads you can make a more informed decision."

"Oh stop it, Gloria. Everything and everyone I love is gone."

"Are they?"

"Yes!"

"What would make you happy?"

"I don't know."

"You do!"

Ruth became more uncomfortable, adjusting her body in the bean bag. She didn't want to hear what Madam La Fong was telling her.

"You must discover what you want for yourself." Madam La Fong continued, "No one can make your choices. You have more money than you know what to do with. Think of people who would give anything to be in your situation; given the opportunity to change their life and direction. You have to let loose, let go of the old, think of something you've always wanted to do, and never had time to do it. Open up, Ruth, you can do it! What is it that you want or need?"

"I spent my entire life here in New York or the Hamptons. I'm a New Yorker. And, now I hate it!"

Madam La Fong observed Ruth showing more signs of being frustrated with the status quo. "Now, we're getting somewhere! What is it that will make you happy?"

"I want to be alone! Away from people," Ruth paused a few moments, "and write my memoirs."

31

"Well, you are not going to be alone here in New York. You said so yourself, you're too well known, everywhere you go, people know you. Privacy and solitude cannot be found here. You must have a place somewhere you can go. Do you?"

Ruth shook her head no.

Madam La Fong continued, "Think of those breadcrumbs that have been laid before you. The answer is right in front of you, and you choose not to see it. Think. Really think about a place where you will have your peace and solitude."

Ruth absorbed what she heard, became less agitated, looked up in deep thought, then around the room at the posters, before she focused on the 1966 Elvis Presley *Blue Hawaii* vintage poster on the wall. Elvis hands out stretched with Diamond Head in the background, seemed to beckon her. She absorbed the palm trees, the beach, Hula girls, the outrigger canoe, and other elements of that vintage *Blue Hawaii* poster. Madam La Fong watched as Ruth experienced her aha moment.

Ruth started to grin; looking almost giddy, nodding, and exclaiming, "The breadcrumbs have been there all along, haven't they? The allure of Hawaii beckons me. The change will be wonderful, won't it?"

* * *

Ruth closed the door to Madam La Fong's and took out her cell phone to call George when it started to ring.

"Hello?" Ruth answered.

"It's George. Good news!"

"Darling, me, too. I'm moving to Hawaii!"

"What? Joe Baccio just made an offer for the property in Hawaii."

"Darling, tell him no and I'll explain it later. I, Ruth Newcomb, am leaving the Big Apple for good and retiring in Hawaii."

"Ruth, you've never been there, not even on a vacation. How do you know you will like it?"

"Sometimes, one must move out of their comfort zone and do something they have never done before; have the courage to take that chance and not be afraid of the unknown."

"But, Ruth!"

"Darling," Ruth continued, "a new door has opened for me, and I am not going to let it close. This is an opportunity of a lifetime that will provide many new challenges and adventures for me. We'll need to arrange to put Beekman Place on the market."

"Ruth, this is a decision you cannot make lightly." George retorted. "Remember how many years it took you to obtain Beekman Place?"

"Darling, I do remember." Reminiscing for a moment, "There is nothing here for me anymore. I want to be alone and want a place to go where no one knows me. Hawaii is the place. Sell Beekman place."

HONOLULU

"We're starting our final approach to Honolulu International Airport. Out the right side of the aircraft is Diamond Head and Waikiki Beach. Please place your seatbacks in an upright position."

Ruth was seated at a first class window seat looking out the window at Diamond Head and Waikiki Beach below.

The plane was still taxiing when a flight attendant announced, "We ask that you remain seated until the captain turns off the seat belt sign. Mahalo."

Another flight attendant approached Ruth.

"Mrs. Newcomb, can you gather your belongings? Please."

Ruth nodded, smiled, and asked, "The captain hasn't turned off the seat belt sign."

"It's okay. You need to deplane first."

Ruth beamed, she was dressed more for attending the opera than for the comfort of flying and glad she was well dressed. She leaned forward and reached under the seat in front of her, pulling out her purse and a nylon pet carrier. Inside, Mrs. Wiggins yellow eyes peer out surveying the passengers. Another flight attendant opened the front

34

cabin door. Ruth got up and followed the flight attendant. The other passengers observed the "special treatment" that Ruth was receiving. A few passengers start to stand up. Another announcement, "Please remain seated until the captain has turned off the seat belt sign. Mahalo."

At the door, a man in a Hawaii Department of Agriculture uniform was waiting for Ruth. "Mrs. Newcomb, can you come with me, please?"

He turned and exited the aircraft followed by Ruth. On the jet way, the officer stopped and turned addressing her. "May I have your pet carrier, please?"

Ruth reluctantly handed over the pet carrier. The officer took the carrier and started to open the jet way door leading to exterior stairs.

"Please be careful, the sun is quite bright." The officer said as he held the door open for Ruth.

"Where are we going?"

"Down to the van."

"Darling, I ordered a limo, not a van."

"Follow me."

"Darling, why aren't we going down the jet way to the terminal?"

"We have business to take care of. Please follow me."

Ruth held her purse up to shield her eyes from the bright sun and followed the officer down the stairs.

"What is going on?" Ruth inquired.

"We're going to the Airport Animal Quarantine holding facility."

"What?"

"I'm here to quarantine your cat. There is a quarantine law to protect our residents and pets from rabies. Hawaii is rabies-free."

"Darling, I can assure you Mrs. Wiggins doesn't have rabies!"

"I'm sure she doesn't."

"You can't quarantine her; she's all I've got!"

"Rules are rules, even in Hawaii."

The airport animal quarantine holding facility looked like any other kennel. Ruth was at the counter, with the officer on the other side with Mrs. Wiggins cat carrier.

"You realize your cat is a little old to be going through something like this."

"Darling, I know, and she is all I have."

"The quarantine law states that your cat must stay in quarantine for 120 days."

"Darling, 120 days?"

"However," the officer responded as he started to smile. "If you have the proper paperwork with you, you would qualify for our five day quarantine."

* * *

In the baggage claim area, a few passengers were still milling about claiming their bags; most were gone. Next to where the bags come out, a door opened as Ruth exited carrying only her purse. She looked around and noticed her Louis Vuitton bags were on baggage carousel. She then spotted a lone limo driver holding a cardboard sign with Mrs. Newcomb professionally printed on it. Ruth went over to him. "Darling, I'm Mrs. Newcomb. My bags are over there."

As the limo made its way through downtown Honolulu, Ruth was transfixed as she observed century old buildings next to modern day ones and how they blended so well together. By the time they reached Waikiki Beach, most of the buildings were modern multistory ones, not unlike New York City, but on a much smaller scale, with palm trees.

The limo pulled up to the modern Halekulani Hotel. A porter, wearing a blue and white hibiscus Aloha shirt and black slacks, opened the limo door for Ruth. On stepping out, she saw the Halekulani hibiscus logo and noticed the fresh smell of the air, along with the aroma of the ocean, and sweet smell of the tropical flora. Another porter took her luggage from the limo placing them on a waiting cart. She observed people wearing muumuu's and Aloha shirts and not walking briskly, but enjoying the sights. Some gave her a nod of recognition as she entered the lobby of the hotel.

* * *

Ruth opened the door to her lanai. The curtains billowed as she went to the handrail to view Diamond Head in the distance, Waikiki Beach, and the hotel pool some ten stories below her corner room. She smiled, nodded with approval; the hotel was virtually no different than what she was accustomed to in any metropolitan city.

She turned her attention to the ocean. In the distance she saw catamarans and surfers catching waves. She smiled and took a deep sigh of relief that she had made the right decision to give up her life in the Manhattan for Hawaii.

* * *

The sun was ready to bid another fond Aloha to Waikiki and the guests at Halekulani's House Without a Key bar; painting the sky a golden hue with orange clouds on the horizon only added to the beauty of the approaching sunset. Ruth, dressed in a designer evening dress, was seated at a table under palm trees swaying with the trade winds, sipping a Manhattan, while other guests enjoyed exotic cocktails with orchids, pineapple, and small umbrella's in them. Everyone enjoyed listening to a trio playing and singing *My Little Grass Shack*. While a woman dressed in an eloquent muumuu performed the Hula to the song. The colors continued to shift as the sunset on the horizon. Ruth remembered the conversations she had with the Martin's about the beauty of the sunset and how Charlie Chan would frequent the very bar she was enjoying.

* * *

The full moon rose behind Diamond Head illuminating Ruth's hotel suite which had tropical flowers strategically placed throughout. A basket of fresh Hawaiian fruits adorned the coffee table. On one wall was a fully stocked bar with assorted glasses. A slight breeze blew the white lace curtains. Ruth looked in her purse, pulled out a piece of paper, and headed for the phone. She dialed the number and waited; there was no answer and she hung up.

* * *

Kalakaua Boulevard, Waikiki's main ocean front street, was crowded with locals and tourists alike, men in shorts and Aloha or T-shirts, while women wore muumuu's or missionary dresses. All are wearing zoris (Hawaiian for flip-flops) for sandals. However, if one individual stood out from the sea of other people, it was Ruth. Ruth walked confidently, wearing a designer dress along with her high heel shoes. Formal or designer dresses and high heels were rarely worn in the tropics; it just wasn't done, except for a special occasion such as a wedding. Even when attending church, missionary dresses or muumuu's are called for, not formal dresses; formal dresses were not the Hawaiian way. No one ever wears high heel shoes in Hawaii except for formal occasions. Most women don't like getting their heels caught in the uneven surfaces or sinking down to their heels in the sand.

Ruth had no real destination in mind, she wanted to see what Hawaii and Waikiki was all about. She was happy people did not stop and ask her for her autograph. They looked, but did not disturb her; Ruth was quite pleased with the freedom Hawaii brought her.

* * *

It was the evening before she could pick up Mrs. Wiggins and fly to the Big Island. She had been unsuccessful in reaching Ben to inform him of her arrival. She tried again waiting for Ben to pick up the phone impatiently waiting. Finally, the phone was picked up.

"Thank God, it's about time." She thought.

"Hello, are you Ben?" Ruth asked, continuing, "Darling, I'm Ruth Newcomb … the new owner.

"Yes, that's right, I'm in Waikiki. I'll be arriving tomorrow on the noon flight.

"Yes, it arrives in Kona at noon. You'll be there, right?

"Good! I'd like a limo with a full bar and sushi.

"I understand. Darling, do what you can do.

"I'm looking forward to meeting you. You'll have a sign so I know who you are, won't you?

"Good! See you then."

Ruth hung up. Hearing the Hawaiian music filtering up from The House Without a Key bar, she walked to the lanai. When she reached the railing, Ruth smiled at the scene around her; the shimmering lights emanating from the city, the full moon rising over Diamond Head with its light shimmering on the ocean surface below. Ruth nodded proclaiming, "No wonder they call this paradise."

THE BIG ISLAND

Ruth wore a fashionable designer dress and her high heel designer shoes, carrying her purse and the pet carrier with Mrs. Wiggins' yellow eyes peering out, making her way past security to the Kona Airport baggage claim area. Many people were being met by lei greeters, a plethora of limo drivers held up signs. Ruth examined each one, and failed to see her name. She continued to look for Ben, and did not see anyone holding a sign resembling anything close to her name. Ruth watched her Louis Vuitton bags pass by as passengers or limo drivers picked up their bags. Being the lone passenger in the baggage claim area, she took each one of her bags to a bench near the exit. Ruth sat looking at her gold Rolex, which read half past noon. Nearby, a tourist magazine rack caught her attention. Getting up, she chose a few including *101 Things to Do on the Big Island* and *The Big Island.* She returned to the bench and started to read *The Big Island.* A little later, she examined her watch which read one o'clock. Looking around, she spotted a pay phone. She left her luggage and headed for the pay phone, reaching into her purse and pulled out a paper and a quarter putting it into the pay phone and dialed the number. After numerous rings, she shook her head and hung up returning to the bench.

A middle aged Hawaiian man, wearing Ray Ban sunglasses, an Aloha shirt, and blue jeans, walked in from the street holding a sheet of lined notebook paper with Luka Newcomb crudely written with a marker.

Ruth could not help but notice her last name and went over to the man who was first to speak. "Aaa-loooo-haa! I am Ben Kokua, are you Mrs. Newcomb?"

"Darling, it's about time! I've been waiting for over an hour. I did say noon, didn't I?" Ruth asked, then pointed to the sign Ben was holding. "Darling, by the way, I'm Ruth Newcomb, not Luka Newcomb."

"Dat okay. You go shi shi, we have long drive."

"Shi shi, what's shi shi?"

"You go baf-room. I wait, watch bags. You go! Baf-room over der."

Ruth left her luggage and cat carrier with Ben and took her purse.

Later, in the Kona Airport parking lot, Ruth followed Ben to the passenger side of a stretch limo as Ben heaved her bags into the back of a rusty mud incrusted blue pickup truck. Ruth looked at the truck dumbfounded. "Darling, we're *not* getting in *that*, are we?"

＊ ＊ ＊

The truck with both windows rolled down, made its way along a long stretch of road high up on the cloudless mountainside, the savannah scattered with parched dried trees in desperate need of water, along with cactus, dried tan grass, lava rocks and flows could be seen for miles in any direction. Every now and then, a goat or two grazed along the roadside. In the distance below, the landscape changed from black of the lava flows and the tan of the parched grass to lush green vegetation nestled along the brilliant deep blue waters of the Pacific.

"Darling, where are the beaches?"

"Da beaches are way down there." Ben replied as he pointed down the hill towards the ocean.

Later, the savannah gave way to plushness; trees and bushes sporadically lined the road. The clear blue sky had given way to menacing rain clouds, as more cars traveled in both directions. On the right side of the truck were cowboys riding horses.

"Darling, look, cowboys!" Ruth exclaimed.

"Paniolo."

"What?"

"Paniolo, dat Hawaiian for cowboy. Dis da Parker Ranch; the largest ranch in the United States."

A light rain started to fall as the truck made its way into a more populated area of one story houses and tropical vegetation. They drove past a rustic wooden sign that announced Waimea, a small town nestled on a plush plateau between two volcanos. They reached a traffic light. While waiting for the light to change, Ruth noticed a strip mall with a large modern supermarket. The light changed, but Ben could only go a few miles an hour due to traffic.

"This traffic is like the states." Ruth declared.

"Dis is Hawaii. We *are* a state."

"Darling, I mean, the traffic shouldn't be like this in paradise. What is going on?"

"Rush hour."

"You have rush hour, here, in Hawaii?"

"Uh, hu! Every day."

"Darling, why, where is everyone going?"

"Shift change."

"Shift change, darling?"

"Dey go to and from da resorts on the sunny side of da island."

The gentle rain gave way to a heavy downpour. Fearing on getting wet, Ruth rolled up her window, while Ben left his down. The truck made its way down a long stretch of road, both sides lined with large trees and lush vegetation. Ben noticed Ruth repeatedly looking out the window visibly bored, looking at her watch, at him, and the cat carrier. Ben attempted to comfort Ruth, "We almost der ... fifteen minute."

The truck slowed down, making an abrupt right onto a smaller one lane road that had seen better days, as it headed up Mauna Kea through sugar cane fields, fertile vegetation, and trees lining the side of the road. The rain had all but abated, giving way to fog which engulfed the freshly rinsed truck. Ruth rolled her window down and was greeted with a very sweet sugary aroma.

"Darling, what is that smell, it is so sweet, smelling almost like sugar or candy."

"It cane. Dat where sugar, molasses, and rum come from."

"You mean that funny stuff that looks like bamboo?" Ruth pointed towards a rogue clump of sugar cane off to the side of the road.

"Uh-huh."

Ruth studied the sugar cane taking in deep sniffs and smiled at the entire scene. The old road by this time had become extremely bumpy, knocking Ruth and Mrs. Wiggins about. To stabilize herself, she grabbed the strap hanging from the roof of the cab above her door; it came off in her hand. She looked at it, then at Ben. With her left hand, she held down the pet carrier as Mrs. Wiggins loudly protested.

The truck slowed down as a car approached them. Ben pulled the truck off to the right to allow the car to pass. As it did so, Ben raised his left hand and waved at the oncoming car, the driver waved back.

Every few hundred yards of the bumpy tree lined road were well paved driveways leading to houses hidden behind the lush tropical rainforest vegetation. Ben made abrupt jerks of the truck to avoid hitting fallen branches, turkeys, or chickens. This combined with the bumpiness made for an extremely uncomfortable ride for Ruth and Mrs. Wiggins.

"Darling, I'm not feeling well." Ben looked at Ruth, whose skin color was slowly turning gray. "I can't take it anymore. All this bouncing around is making me unwell." The truck continued to bounce.

"Darling, stop the truck now! I'm going to be sick!"

The truck turned into a ginger and tree lined impeccably maintained driveway and stopped. Ruth opened the door and stuck her head out about ready to throw up, but quickly regained her composure. She looked down the driveway where she saw an inviting beautiful blue and white trimmed three car garage. Behind it, was a larger modern blue and white trimmed house with a matching blue metal roof.

"What a beautiful house!" Ruth exclaimed.

"In Hawaii, we say hale for house."

"I must start to learn new Hawaiian words. Darling, do you know who lives there?"

"Uh-huh. You do."

HALE NEWCOMB

Ben pulled the truck closer to the garage and parked. He retrieved the luggage and walked towards the house. Ruth reached for the carrying case, looked inside to find a shivering and cowering Mrs. Wiggins in the back, tail twitching.

"It's okay, Mrs. Wiggins." Upon hearing the Ruth's calming voice, Mrs. Wiggins moved forward. Ruth turned the carrier away from her, sharing the surrounding terrain with Mrs. Wiggins.

"Darling, we live here, isn't this wondrous?"

Ruth followed Ben down the concrete and grass pathway leading from the garage to the house. She was more enthralled with the beauty of the scenery around her than walking when she accidently stepped into the grassy section which caused her heel to slightly sink into the grass. She momentarily lost her balance causing the cat carrier to violently swing. Mrs. Wiggins let out a curt sorrowful meow. Ruth quickly regained her balance. paying more attention to where she was walking as she continued to follow Ben towards the main house.

Beyond the house, a vast macadamia nut orchard came into view. A variety of citrus trees with large fruit line the boundary between the front yard and the orchard. Chickens, wild turkey, and néné (Hawaiian geese) pecked the ground. Upon hearing Ruth and Ben approaching, the birds scurried for protection in the orchard and adjacent vegetation.

The blue house was encircled by a large lanai which wrapped the uphill exterior. Without using a key, Ben opened the front door and held it open. Ruth walked in, the downhill view from the living room floor to ceiling windows caught her attention. She walked over to examine the view. Through the trees, in the distance, she saw the unmistakable dark blue waters of the Pacific and smiled. Ben walked up behind her.

"Nice view, isn't it?" Ben inquired.

Ruth nodded, "Darling, this is truly paradise."

Ben started towards Ruth's bedroom, down a short hallway off the living room. "I put your stuff in da master suite. If you need me, I live in the other end of the house." Ben pointed down a longer hallway.

Ruth placed the pet carrier on the wooden floor and opened its door to free Mrs. Wiggins who darted out heading down the shorter hallway where Ben had gone. Upon hearing the unfamiliar sounds Ben was making, she abruptly stopped and skidded as she made a U-turn and returned to the carrier.

A few moments later, Ben returned to the living room where Ruth had focused her attention to the lanai and uphill scenery of the fog making its way towards the house. Ruth was so enamored with the scenery outside she started for the front door.

"You need Cutter." Ben told Ruth as she opened the door. She had not heard him and continued to go outside and took in the view of the orchard and the fauna; mango, orange, lime, lemon, and other fruit trees scattered around. Ginger, bird of paradise, and anthurium plants define the separation of house and orchard. She took a deep breath and smiled.

Through the living room window, Ben watched Ruth, who was experiencing great difficulty walking and maintaining her balance due to her high heel shoes sinking into the grass. Suddenly Ruth started swatting the air around her as though she was being attacked by something. She started to slap her exposed arms and legs. Ben headed to the kitchen as Ruth was trying to maintain her balance as she returned the house. When she entered the kitchen, Ben held out the can of Cutter's bug spray.

"Darling, you didn't tell me about the mosquitoes. What is the can for?"

"It rain a lot here. Spray Cutter on skin, den da bug no bite. Da haole need Cutter's."

Ruth cocked her head mouthing the word haole.

"Haole," Ben explained, "dat mean white people or tourist."

* * *

Ruth was asleep wearing a silk eye night mask with Mrs. Wiggins curled against her. The tranquil sounds of Mrs. Wiggins snoring, the crickets chirping, and coqui frogs croaking had abruptly given way to muted sounds of popping, which remotely sounded like the backfire of a car, followed by loud grunting sounds had awakened Ruth. She removed her night mask and looked at the clock which revealed 4:31. She sat upright and listened to the popping and grunting sounds appearing to be coming from another room or outside. She grabbed Mrs. Wiggins and held her close, stroking her.

"Darling, at least they are not in our room. This is Hawaii not New York! I'm sure we're going to be alright."

Ruth continued her watch for about a quarter of an hour or so when the grunting sounds abated and gave way once again to the gentle sounds of the crickets and frogs. Ruth was still seated upright in bed holding and gently stroking a purring Mrs. Wiggins. She returned Mrs. Wiggins to her spot before replacing the silk night mask and lay down.

The peacefulness of night gave way to dawn which was announced by a lone rooster crowing, startling Ruth and Mrs. Wiggins. Ruth removed her mask, looked around, and realized it was her first morning in the country of the Big Island. The rooster continued crowing; others joining in, welcoming the rising sun and a new day.

* * *

Ruth was seated at the kitchen table sipping a cup of coffee reading *The Big Island,* one of the throw-away magazines. On the cover was a photograph of a black sand beach, with palm trees, and waterfall cutting its way down a large cliff in the background. Ben entered and poured himself a cup of coffee.

"How did you sleep?" Ben inquired.

Ruth put the magazine down.

"Sleep? Darling, I was awakened by your grunting."

"Grunt? I no grunt."

"Then what was that sound if it wasn't you."

"It da pig!"

Ruth cocked her head and gave Ben an inquisitive look.

"Wild boar." Ben continued, "Dey come for the mac nut and mango. Not every night, some night, when dey get hungry."

"Darling, nothing can be that loud when eating."

"Look under tree, you see big dirt area, that done by pig. De laikem mac nut."

"Laikem what is laikem?"

"It Pidgin for like them. You know, laik-em! Pidgin easy to speak."

"Darling, you did a fantastic job of unpacking and arranging my belongings before my arrival. The house looks like I've lived here for some time. Thank you."

"You're welcome. I thought you would like it."

Ruth nodded and returned her attention to the magazine, then back to Ben.

"Darling, I want to go shopping and see the island."

"I drive you."

"I want to do it myself. I want a car."

"You take truck."

Ruth shook her head. "I do not do trucks, I can barely drive cars."

"You need four wheel drive. Truck mo betta."

"Darling, I said I don't do trucks. You have to find me a car."

THE NEIGHBORS

Ruth was in the living room watering plants when the front door burst open without a knock as Auntie, a jubilant robust mid-sixty year old Hawaiian-Asian dressed in a muumuu and wearing zoris, entered. Ruth was so startled by Auntie's abrupt entrance, she dropped the glass Tiffany pitcher which shattered across the living room tile floor.

"Oh! You clumsy lady," Auntie exclaimed in singsong Hawaiian pidgin. "Where Ben? He kokua you, klinim mess, den he kam my place. Da keiki's need him. Where he?"

"Darling, who are you?"

"Me? I Auntie."

"Who ... what gives you the right to burst into my house without knocking?"

"Ben wok fo me."

"Darling, he works for me!"

"Oh, dat oh-kay."

"No, it's not okay."

"When you see Ben, tell him, come plenny wikiwiki." Auntie commanded.

A moment later, Ben came running from the back of the house into the living room.

"Oh, der you are!" Auntie exclaimed, addressing Ben, "Da keiki's need you. You klinim here first." Pointing to the broken Tiffany pitcher. "Den kam wikiwiki." She turned for the door and abruptly disappeared.

"Darling, what was that all about?" Ruth asked.

"What?" Ben inquired.

"That lady, what is with her?"

"Dat Auntie. I work for her, too."

"I don't like the way she just burst into my house. I want to be left alone."

"I talk to her."

* * *

Ben entered the interior of a large opaque plastic greenhouse Quonset hut. The aroma of a freshly mowed lawn with a hint of a skunk permeated the building. An elaborate watering system hung from the metal frame of the greenhouse. Auntie was trimming one of several hundred marijuana plants; most had reached maturity.

"A-lo-ha." Ben said as he entered.

"A-lo-ha, she plenny tight!"

"Oh, she oh-kay. She da new owner. She no like her name Luka ... she like Ruth." Ben picked up a pair of trimming shears and started to trim one of the plants near Auntie.

"Luka, Hawaiian name. Ruth, haole name. She plenny haole. Ruth, mo betta." Auntie stroked one of the plants, adding, "da keiki, dey nidim our kokua nau."

* * *

Ruth, wearing a sundress with house slippers, was seated on one of the Adirondack chairs on her lanai typing on her laptop. A can of Cutter's bug spray was on the table. The sun beamed on a curled up Mrs. Wiggins who was on the grass at the foot of the steps. The brightness of the sun yielded to a darkness Ruth had never experienced. It started to lightly rain, followed almost immediately by a downpour. Mrs. Wiggins' tail twitched as she looked up at Ruth and let out a long sorrowful meow which was drowned out by the deafening sound of the rain hitting the metal roof. Ruth jumped up and ran for the cat, reaching her in moments. As Ruth bent down and grabbed the cat, she heard a loud roaring, rumbling sound, coming down the hill towards her. She looked towards the sound to see a foot high torrent of water, mud, branches, flowing in her direction. Ruth being unable to maintain her balance fell backward landing on her derrière. The torrent was so powerful, Ruth and the cat started to slide down the hill.

Ruth continued to slide, holding the caterwauling cat up in the air. They were carried down the hill plowing through a thicket of bushes, her mud covered sundress moved up to her thighs. She saw she was about to hit a house and braced her legs for impact, holding the mud covered cat close to her. They slammed into the side of the house which shook as though a boulder hit it.

The downpour continued as Nalani and Meka, the middle aged Hawaiian-Filipino owners of the house downhill from Ruth, ran to the uphill side of their house to see what caused the huge thump, only to find Ruth and the cat covered with mud. Ruth looked up.

Nalani looked at Ruth, "rain stop soon."

Meka reached down and helped Ruth up.

"Eh, wha? Ohhh!" Ruth exclaimed.

"We wait on lanai for rain to stop. Then you can go." Nalani suggested as they walked to their lanai. The rain was so heavy, it washed the mud off both Ruth and Mrs. Wiggins.

Nalani escorted them to four rickety chairs surrounding a table on the lanai. "You sit."

"I'm Meka." Meka said, before pointing to Nalani. "Dis Nalani, da misses."

"Darlings, it is nice to meet you. I'm Ruth Newcomb, I live next door, up the hill. Does it always rain like this?"

"Dis sometimes happens when da rains are in da right place on Mauna Kea. Da good ding is, it doesn't last too long." Meka answered.

Nalani looked at Ruth's slippers, then up at Ruth. "No won-da you fall. House slippahs no good in Hawaii, too slippery. You need zori."

"Zori?"

"Haole call dem flip-flops."

I NEED A CAR!

The bright Hawaiian sun filtered through the floor to ceiling kitchen nook windows where Ruth and Ben were having their morning coffee.

"Darling, have you found a car yet?" Ruth inquired.

"Yes."

"Where is it?"

"It not ready."

"Why not?"

"No windows."

"Darling, what good is a car without an windows?"

"Dat is all I could find. You take truck?"

"Ben, I don't want to use your truck. I want to own my own car. Where do we go to get a car? One with windows?"

"Hilo, it closer than Kona."

"Fine, we go to Hilo and buy a car."

"Auntie need me."

"She can wait. I need a car, now!"

* * *

The car dealership was small compared to those found on the mainland, with one or two of each vehicle model. Ruth was still dressed more like a mainlander, wore a designer dress and high heels, was with Ben and a car salesman looking the small selection of cars.

"Not many cars have four wheel drive," the salesman said, "you really need a truck or SUV."

"I don't want a truck. What is an SUV?" Ruth inquired.

"Sports Utility Vehicle. Dey like a truck, but look like a cross between a van and a car, and a lot more comfortable." The salesman took Ruth and Ben over to a couple of SUV's. "Dis one will get you from Hilo to Kona on Saddle Road, like riding in first class. No bouncing, smooth ride. It's great when you get caught in downpour. You can go almost anywhere on the island."

"Darling, what about Waipio Valley?"

The salesman shook his head. "These are All Wheel Drive SUV's, they may not make it. You need a four wheel drive SUV. Let's go over here."

The salesman took Ruth and Ben to a four wheel drive black SUV "Dis da best SUV to use. You won't slide off the road like other SUV's and trucks do when you go down to Waipio."

"Okay, I'll buy it." Astonished, both Ben and the salesman look at Ruth, "On one condition, you show me how to operate it."

"It's easy. But first, you must always take off your high heels when you engage da four wheel drive. Safety first."

Ruth got into the driver's seat and took off her high heels as the salesman got into the passenger's seat and gave instructions on the operation of the gears and pedals. Ben stood nearby watching the training session unfold. Before long the sound of the SUV starting was heard, followed by the wrenching sound of grinding gears. This was repeated several times before the grinding sound was followed by the SUV lurching forward and coming to an abrupt stop.

Ben looked on, shaking his head wondering if Ruth would ever be able handle the SUV. After an hour of training, Ruth was able to drive the vehicle around the lot with little trepidation and parked in front of Ben.

* * *

A pleasant breeze blew down Mauna Kea rustling through the macadamia orchard teemed with a variety chickens, turkeys, and néné's pecking the grass. Occasionally the sound was interrupted by a crowing cock. Mrs. Wiggins was curled up on one of the Adirondack chairs on the lanai. Ruth was typing away on the laptop. "If you ever saw *The Trouble with Angels* with Haley Mills and June Harding; that would typify my schooling at St. Francis Academy for Girls. I was more the Haley character where Sarah Martin was June's. As in the movie, we had fun devising schemes to be defiant. Even to this day, I don't like rulers; they remind me of the nuns using the back of our hands for target practice."

As Ruth continued to type, she heard pecking near the bottom of the lanai steps. She looked up and saw a couple of wild turkeys had made their way to Mrs. Wiggins' cat food dish eating its contents. The chickens and néné followed the turkey's lead and made their way to the dish and water. Ruth bolted from her chair frantically waving her arms. "Shoo, shoo!" The birds scurried into the orchard. Mrs. Wiggins disinterestedly looked up at the commotion and returned to her nap.

HONOKA'A

Honoka'a Town was the closest village with a post office. Almost every sign in town had an accent between the two a's. Locals and tourists alike left the pronunciation of the second "a" off saying Honokaa in lieu of Honoka'a. This was quite acceptable to most, however, those true to the old Hawaiian ways would always pronounce the second a.

In the center of Honoka'a, the paint had peeled on a majority of the wooden buildings. The aged elevated wooden sidewalk had an occasional missing board that made it hard to walk on, while the newer sections were made of concrete. The dilapidated sugar mill wasn't far from town. When the mill was in operation, the workers and towns' people used to hang out at Mr. Woo's, the only market for miles around. There was no doubt Honoka'a had seen better days. However, the town was going through a Renaissance. The government recently built a modern brick post office down the street from Mr. Woo's.

A breeze blew through the open aired post office box collection area. Ruth, wearing a designer dress and high heel shoes, was collecting mail from her post office box.

The only other person in the post office box collection area was Danny Mauka, the local television station manager. Danny knew everyone and what was happening on the north end of the island. He smiled at Ruth as she walked past him, "What a wonderful dress you are wearing. Where's the wedding?"

"Wedding?" Ruth inquisitively replied. "Darling, why would I be going to a wedding? I am picking up my mail."

"Sorry, I thought there was a wedding that I wasn't aware of. People always tell me when there is a wedding or other big event."

"Darling, sorry to disappoint you." Ruth responded and continued to walk down the street to Mr. Woo's Market which was not much larger than a mainland convenience store. Inside were a variety of items, primarily small single use or sample size items, one of almost everything. Ruth walked through the aisles looking for peanut butter. Finally, she spotted a small jar. She picked it up and looked at it. She frowned and shook her head thinking one would be lucky to get a couple of peanut butter and jelly sandwiches out of such a small jar. Ruth went to the front of the store to the sole cash register. Nearby, Mr. Woo, an older Asian man, wore a white apron stocking shelves. As Ruth approached him, he bowed, "How may I help you?"

"Darling, do you have a larger jar of peanut butter?" Ruth asked.

"Have only small. Big ones at da supermarket in Waimea."

* * *

Waimea was about fifteen miles up the main road from Mr. Woo's. Ruth pulled her SUV into a parking space at the large Waimea supermarket. When she got out of the

SUV, she was beaming and proud that she made the half hour journey herself without incident.

Mr. Woo was right, the supermarket was enormous. Locals and tourists alike pushed their carts through the large well stocked aisles. The tourists could be readily identified because they were tanner than the locals and had crackers, nuts, and other fattening snacks and liquor in their carts. Ruth roamed the aisles looking at all the unfamiliar local items and the mainland brand name items she was so familiar with. When she reached the peanut butter and jelly aisle, she was amazed by the large variety of local fruits and vegetables that were made into jams, jellies, and preserves next to the peanut butter.

Charlene, a lightly tanned copper haired woman in a missionary dress with kitschy Hello Kitty zoris, was visually sorting through the variety of peanut butter jars. Ruth saw there was only one jumbo jar of peanut butter left on the shelf. At the same moment, Ruth and Charlene reached for that sole jumbo jar. However, Ruth was the first to grab it.

"I was reaching for that jar." Charlene exclaimed.

"Darling, it's my peanut butter." Ruth selfishly responded.

Charlene examined the overdressed Ruth from head to toe.

"Your first time on the island, isn't it?"

"Darling, I live here!"

Without maintaining eye contact, Charlene scanned the shelves and found and took a smaller peanut butter container. Looking back at Ruth, Charlene decided she would defuse the conflict stating, "A long time ago, I was like you."

"Darling, I *am* the only one like me." Ruth exclaimed.

Charlene shook her head and extended her hand. "I'm Charlene Strong, Honokaa's high school counselor." Ruth refused to shake hands. "When I first arrived from the mainland, I too used to be uptight like you. We are now

59

on the Big Island, not the mainland. Life is different here. In time, you too will change and become more relaxed and enjoy our Big Island ways."

Without wanting nor needing to respond to Charlene, Ruth turned and left her, who responded, "Have a great day, A-lo-ha!"

DOESN'T ANYBODY KNOCK?

While Ruth was shopping in Waimea, William Ayala, teenage son of Nalani and Meka, Ruth's neighbors, was carrying a Hawaiian floral arrangement of anthuriums and birds of paradise in a glass vase, opened Ruth's unlocked front door. After William placed the arrangement on the living room coffee table, he looked around the room and noticed changes Ruth had made to the Martin's former home. He noticed the photographs of Ruth with the Clinton's and Donald Trump, Jackie Onassis, Princess Dianna and Prince Charles in the book case. He spotted the Emmy placed in the center of the book case. Having only seen one on television, he went to the shelf and studied it up close. William remembered that many of the actors said how heavy the Emmy was, so he decided he would pick it up and almost dropped it because it indeed was heavy. He examined the gold statuette and the plaque that read "Outstanding Informational Series - 2001, Ruth Newcomb - Host, *From the Big Apple*", and then returned it to its resting place, turning his attention to the collection of hardback books which include *The Adventures of Tom Sawyer, The Adventures of Huckleberry Finn, Catcher in the Rye,*

Uncle Tom's Cabin amongst Dante, Dickens, and other classics.

William looked at the flowers, "Des no gut here." He picked up the flower arrangement and headed for the kitchen where he placed it on the center of the island making sure everything looked perfect. He returned to the living room to leave and found Ruth was entered through the front door with her paper bag of groceries. Ruth screamed and dropped her bag.

"What are you doing here?"

William innocently replied, "Noth-thing."

"You are stealing something, aren't you?"

William shook his head no.

Ben came running in from the front door and noticed William, "William, what are you doing here?"

"Noth-thing."

"You go home."

William started to leave.

"No!" Ruth proclaimed, "I want to know what he is doing here."

"I do noth-thing."

"Darling, you are here. That's enough."

"I do noth-thing, I just leaving."

Ben did not want to further escalate the situation and commanded, "William, you go."

As William headed for the door, Ruth scolded him, "Darling, where I come from people just don't wander into other peoples' homes. It's a violation."

When William reached the door, Auntie burst into the room addressing Ben and William, "You come, wikiwiki! Da keiki's no wait!"

"I go." William responded as he left.

Auntie observed the bag on the floor, "You fo'ever drop dings."

Ruth gave Auntie a look of disdain.

"I no like yu stink-eye. I go."

Auntie turned and left the house leaving Ben and Ruth alone in the living room.

"Talk about violations! People enjoy popping in around here, don't they?"

"Uh-huh."

"Darling, what are those keiki things that lady is always talking about? Why are they so important?"

"Keiki, it Hawaiian for little ones or children. If everything oh-kay, I go Auntie's."

Ruth watched Ben leave and head up the hill to Auntie's. After picking up the grocery bag, Ruth went to the kitchen and placed the bag next to the flower arrangement on the kitchen island. She reached for the yellow rotary wall phone and picked up the receiver, then hung up. Opening a cabinet door, she pulled out a worn AT&T telephone book and placed it on the island and then noticed the flower arrangement. She smiled, thinking Ben had put the arrangement on the island. Ruth returned her attention to the telephone book and noticed that it had the original AT&T logo of years past. She shook her head, opened the book, and looked at the inside the cover, picked up the phone and dialed the number, "Police?"

* * *

Later that same day, Ruth was reading Dante's *Purgatory* in the living room. She heard footsteps coming from the lanai before the front door burst open. Two police officers entered. Ruth was startled. "What the heck! Doesn't anyone knock around here?" Hearing no answer, "I'm glad you are here."

"You want to report a break in?" The first officer queried.

"Darling, why else would I have called you?"

The second officer attempted to be funny and lighten the tension asked, "What was broken?"

Ruth saw no humor in the question, "I want to report a break in. I even know who he is and where he lives. He's the neighbor boy next door."

The officers looked at each other and smiled.

"Oh, William ... William Ayala, he's harmless. He won't cause you no harm. He's a curious kid."

"I don't like it that he was in *my* house. In New York this isn't done."

"Dis is Hawaii, not New York." The first officer countered.

"Did you lock da door before you left?"

"Yes, and Ben, my caretaker, also lives here."

"So maybe Ben didn't lock da door?"

"I don't know."

"No harm done. Nothing taken. Is der anything else you need?"

"Darling, I want something done."

"There isn't anything for us to do if nothing was taken."

Ruth shook her head.

The first officer looked to the second officer, "We're here, we check on Auntie."

* * *

Ruth was seated in her white Adirondack chair on the lanai reading *The New Yorker* magazine. Ben was coming down the hill from Auntie's. As he approached the lanai, Ruth asked, "Ben, come here, please."

Ben walked over to Ruth and took a seat on the other Adirondack chair.

"Darling, I don't want to be disturbed. I want to be left alone."

Ben started to rise. "You want me to leave?"

"No, Ben, sit."

Ben sat back down.

"What I don't like," Ruth continued, "is everyone keeps bursting into my house not knocking. From Auntie, to the police, to William. So, I want you to install a security system." Ruth laid down *The New Yorker* displaying an elaborate security system advertisement and showed it to Ben. "Like this one."

"Door has lock."

"No, Ben, I want a security system."

"Dis Hawaii, nobody has security system."

"Darling, I don't care if we are in Timbuktu. When can you install it?"

Ben scratched his head, "I don't know where to get security system."

Ruth pointed to the phone number on the advertisement, "Here's the number. I want it done. Do you understand?"

Ben nodded.

WAIPIO VALLEY

The aroma of coffee filled the kitchen as Ruth and Ben finished their morning brew. She looked at the flower arrangement.

"Ben, I forgot to thank you for the nice flowers."

"Flowers? I thought you put them there."

"I wonder how they got here."

Ruth and Ben inquisitively look at each other when Ben realized what happened.

"Dat what he do here!"

"Who?"

"William."

Ruth looked at the flowers and smiled.

"Darling, why didn't he tell us?"

"You scare him."

"He scared me! That was very kind of him."

Ruth looked down at *The Big Island* throw-away magazine which had a photograph of the Waipio Valley on the cover.

"Darling, is Waipio Valley as breathtaking as these photographs?"

"Uh-huh."

"How long does it take to get there?"

"Too dangerous to drive, you hike."

"Hike from where?"

"You park at top, hike down to beach. Da hike takes half an hour to get down, over an hour to go up."

"I have an SUV, I can drive."

"Some people don't make it."

"The salesman told me I could do it!"

"Oh-kay, use only first gear and drive very slowly. Going down is hard; going up easy. You need carrots with stalk attached."

Ruth gave Ben an inquisitive look. "Carrots?"

"You need carrots when you get to bottom." Ben got up. "I go to Auntie's."

* * *

Ruth dressed in a designer outfit and high heel shoes, double checked the front door, making sure that it was locked. She nodded and smiled.

Later she exited Mr. Woo's holding a bunch of carrots by the stalk heading for her SUV and drove to the entrance at the top of Waipio Valley. The sun was shining brightly, not a cloud to be seen. The parking lot was filled with cars. The road ahead of her had barriers on both sides, narrowing down from the two lane well paved road to a one lane paved road that has seen better days. A large sign on one side of the road stated, *STOP, Restricted Road, Only 4-wheel Drive Vehicles Permitted, One lane road, Downhill traffic must yield to uphill traffic.* On the other side was another sign, *WARNING, proceed at your own risk, Steep Grade, Engage all wheels, Engage first gear, Falling rock.* Ruth studied the signs making the final decision as to go ahead with her plan and traverse the over half mile road down to the valley floor.

Ruth reached down and took off her high heel shoes, looked at the gears and shifted the SUV into first gear. She pulled gently away and started driving extremely slowly down the very steep potholed one lane road. Ruth was so intent on driving and staying on the road, avoiding the tourists hiking single file down the steep narrow road, she doesn't notice the beautiful fertile valley and beach below. She was happy no one was driving up the one lane road without a guardrail, as she wasn't sure how much room the two vehicles would have without one of them going off the steep cliff into the valley below.

Ten arduous minutes later, Ruth finally reached the bottom of the precipice where there was a small area wide enough for two vehicles before the road made an abrupt hairpin U-turn towards the beach. She stopped and took a long deep breath, happy she had made it without falling off the road into the valley.

Regaining her composure, Ruth started driving again, this time following the road into the darkness of thick overgrowth of tropical foliage. It took a few moments for her eyes to adjust on going from the brightness into the deep darkness of dense tropical jungle before her. The road had also changed, it was no longer paved, but an unpaved muddy potholed road. As she continued driving, occasionally light streamed through the thickness of towering trees helping to illuminate the road in before her.

Still in first gear, Ruth made her way down the road, trying to avoid the water filled potholes the size of Volkswagen Beetles and the occasional tourist walking the same direction she was going. She reached a somewhat dry flat area and decided to take a few moments to rest and check out the jungle that surrounded her. To her right, a stream of light filtering through the trees illuminated the hull of a rusted car smashed against a tree. Ruth noticed a tree was between the car and the road. Furthermore, the car was on its side with the wheels facing the road. It is then Ruth realized that the car came from the road above her; the same road she had traversed not minutes before.

While gazing upward into the trees, Ruth saw a rusted carcass of a pickup truck perched in one tree. Looking around, she spotted a car and another and another. The trees were adorned with rusted cars and trucks that didn't make it.

After a few moments, Ruth regained her composure and started driving again, following the muddy pothole infused road which eventually opened up to a sandy path leading through the pine and palm trees where other SUV's and trucks were parked. Wondering amongst the palms and trees were a dozen wild horses. She found a grassy part between two palm trees and parked. She reached down to put on her high heel shoes. Five horses started to meander towards the SUV unnoticed by Ruth. She got out and reached into the SUV, grabbed the carrots, and closed the door. As Ruth turned, she found herself encircled by the horses. She then understood why Ben told her to take carrots with stalks. Ruth took a carrot, held it by the stalk and cautiously extended it towards one of the horses who gently took it from her. She was jubilant; smiling to the point of almost laughing. She took another carrot, again holding it by the stalk; another horse took it from her. The five horses had her pinned against the SUV whinnying and nuzzling Ruth as she continued to feed them. She quickly ran out of carrots and held both hands up showing the horses that she doesn't have any more.

"All gone."

At which point, the horses turned, leaving the SUV. A few moments later, more horses approached. Again, she held her hands up.

"My little darlings, I have no more, all gone."

The horses whinnied and meandered away; no doubt searching for their next victim.

Ruth started to walk down to the gray/black beach. The moment she stepped off of the grassy area, her shoes sank deeply into the sand. Ruth was trapped, unable to move. It took some effort to slide out of the heels and go barefoot. She carried her shoes with her as she headed to the beach to watch the waves crashing along the shoreline.

The secluded bay was perfect for surfing and a few locals were enjoying the surf. The occasional tourist who had hiked down to the beach were cooling off in the refreshing water. Ruth thought to herself this was what Hawaii was like before all the big resort hotels and people came to the islands. The gentle trade winds rustled the palm trees causing Ruth to turn her attention to the land behind her. To her right, a river flowed into the ocean. To her left, a waterfall cascaded some fifteen hundred feet down into the Pacific. It looked oddly familiar and then she remembered Kevin Costner telling her and her television audience about the shooting of the last scene of *Waterworld* in Waipio Valley. She took a deep breath, sighed, and smiled at all the peacefulness and tropical beauty.

* * *

Ruth was driving back into the jungle, doing a good job of navigating the potholes and occasional tourist walking along the muddy road. In front of her, she saw the bright light shining through the trees indicating the journey through the darkness of the jungle was coming to an end. She made it into the sunlight and the last flat area before she had to make the sharp hairpin U-turn to traverse up the very steep one lane road back to civilization. Ruth took a moment to gather her wits before attempting to make the return trip up to the top of the cliff. She took a deep breath, looked at the clutch, put it into first gear, and pressed the gas pedal, as she released the clutch with her left foot, the gears ground a bit, as the SUV started moving slowly forward. There was a loud thud.

Ruth realized the SUV had struck something and she slammed on the brakes. She was sure there wasn't anything in front of the SUV before she started studying the gears. She looked up to see the body of a young man was on the hood of the SUV and put the SUV into park, got out, and went to the man, his face still facing the hood of the SUV.

"Darling, are you okay? I'm so sorry."

The man looked up at Ruth. It was William.

"I am oh-kay, Mrs. Newcomb."

"Darling, I didn't see you there. I'm so sorry. You aren't going to sue me, are you?"

"Huh?"

"Are you going to sue me?"

"Why would I sue you?"

"I'm from New York, everybody sues."

"I won't sue you. Can you give me a lift to da top?"

"Yes..."

Ruth started to get into the driver's seat.

"Darling, are you *sure* you're not hurt?"

"I am alright."

William got into the passenger seat. Ruth slowly drove the SUV up the Waipio Valley cliff road very intent on not becoming its next victim, as they both bounced all over the place.

* * *

The SUV had successfully made it to the top of the cliff.

"Darling, do you need a ride home?"

"No, Mrs. Newcomb, Honokaa would be fine. Thank you for the offer"

They were back on a well paved two lane road going through sugarcane fields where the sweet aroma did not go unnoticed by Ruth. The sugarcane fields were interspersed with an occasional house or two off to the side of the road. William looked out the open window at the cane fields.

"Darling, about yesterday." Ruth paused, "Thank you for the flowers."

"You're welcome."

"You know you shouldn't go uninvited into other people's homes, right?"

"Uh-huh."

"Darling, it's not right intruding like that."

"I'm sorry, Mrs. Newcomb."

More houses were coming into view as they approached Honoka'a. William slinked down into the seat. He was almost on the floor. They were approaching Honoka'a High School.

Mrs. Strong, the school counselor, was standing at the curb; arms folded looking down the street as the SUV approached. Ruth looked down at William, "There's no need for you to be down there."

After the SUV passed the school, William moved back up into his seat.

"William, aren't you still in high school?"

"Uh-huh."

"Then why aren't you in class?"

"I don't like English. I go to beach instead."

"Darling, you need English. School is important."

"Dat what Mrs. Strong, my counselor, says."

The SUV made a U-turn, heading back towards the school.

"What are you doing?" William frantically exclaimed.

"Darling, I am taking you to school."

"I don't want to go!"

The SUV pulled up to the school. William got out looking at the ground as he approached Mrs. Strong.

"Hello, Mrs. Strong."

Ruth listened to the conversation through the open window.

"William, you're early today. How was da beach?"

"It oh-kay."

"William, you get to Dr. Tilton's class. He's expecting you."

Mrs. Strong leaned down, looking into the passenger window. Both Ruth and Mrs. Strong instantly recognized each other.

"It's you!" Mrs. Strong exclaims. "Thank you for bringing William. At least he'll be able to catch part of his English class. Forgot to tell you the other day at the market, this may be The Big Island, however, we are a tight little island; one where everyone knows everyone else and what goes on. Thank you for bringing him to school, you performed a great service."

DA GHOST OF AN OLD KAHUNA

A heavy fog engulfed the area as Ruth was on her lanai typing away on her the laptop. Ruth heard a noise and looked up to see who it was, however, the fog was so thick, she started to pick up the laptop to go inside when recognized it was William and put the laptop back down.

"Aaa-loooo-haa, Mrs. Newcomb. What are you doing?"

"I am writing my memoirs."

"Why?"

"Darling, I had a wonderful life and people will love to read it. How did it go in school today?"

"Oh-kay. I got to help Auntie with her keiki's." William started to walk up to Auntie's, looked over his shoulder saying, "Aaa-loooo-haa!"

* * *

As Ruth walked through the macadamia orchard, her slippers sank into the thick grass. Beneath the trees, mac nuts covered the ground. She frowned and shook her head. She turned to head towards the house when she saw Ben had started up the hill towards Auntie's, "Ben!"

He does not hear Ruth.

Ruth yelled louder, "Ben!" He turned. "I need to talk to you." When he reached Ruth, she continued, "Darling, how is it going with the security system?"

"Ah, I still look for one."

"It shouldn't take this long to locate a system."

"Dis Hawaii, take long time to get stuff."

"You've been spending too much time with Auntie."

Ashamed, Ben looked towards the ground.

"No, I haven't."

"Look at this place." Ruth made a sweeping motion with her hand. "The grass needs mowing."

Ben looked around at the overly long uncut grass, "Uh-huh."

"Look at all the nuts under the trees, they need to be collected and sold."

"Uh-huh."

"The Martin's raved about how good of a caretaker you are. Darling, I just haven't seen it."

"I sorry, da keiki's need attention. Dey no wait."

"Darling, I know the children, I mean the keiki's, need attention and so do my macadamia nut trees and the lawn. Please take care of it this week."

"Oh-kay."

Auntie came down the hill towards Ruth and Ben. She went up to Ben, "Oh, der you are!" Then turned her attention to Ruth, "How you?"

"I'm fine. I need Ben to spend more time with me."

"No, he need to spend time wit me and da keiki's. Dey important right now."

"Darling, my lawn and macadamia nuts are important too."

"Da mac nut wait. Keiki's no wait. Ben, you come."

Auntie started up the hill followed by Ben.

"This week, Ben!"

Ben looked over his shoulder, "Uh-huh."

* * *

Ruth, in her designer dress and high heels, drove down the two lane road towards Honoka'a Town. A lone hitchhiker came into view, it was William. She pulled over, "Get in."

"Aaa-looo-haaa, Mrs. Newcomb."

William got into the car.

"Going to school, William?"

"No, Waipio."

"Why don't you want to go to school?"

"Dr. Tilton makes us read aloud. It embarrasses me."

"There is nothing to be embarrassed about. Public speaking is easy."

"Dr. Tilton is not human! People say he is da ghost of an old kahuna."

"Darling, Dr. Tilton cannot be all that bad."

"He is!" William exclaimed, "He makes us read da big words."

The SUV approached the school.

"When I lived in New York, I used to volunteer to help people learn to read. I can do the same for you, William."

William looked at Ruth and smiled.

"I want you to go to Dr. Tilton's class." William frowned, as Ruth continued, "Try your best, then after school, I want you to come to my place and we will work on your reading."

William smiled, "Sometimes, Auntie helps me, too."

Ruth stopped the SUV at the front of the school.

William got out and went to the front walkway of the school. He looked over his shoulder.

Ruth was watching.

William continued walking and opened the front door. He looked over his shoulder again.

Ruth was watching.

William entered, the door closed. Through the front door window William looked out. The door opened as Mrs. Strong stepped out, mouthed thank you and waved at Ruth.

READING IS AN ADVENTURE

The light streamed onto the lanai as Ruth typed away on her laptop. On the table next to her was *Time Magazine* with a publicity photo of her on the cover, the headline in red lettering read *From The Big Apple No More, A Tradition Dies*.

William walked through the orchard and approached Ruth. "Aaa-looo-haaa, Mrs. Newcomb."

"Hello, William."

William noticed Ruth's photograph on the cover of *Time Magazine*.

"That's you, isn't it?"

"Yes, darling."

"Why is your picture on da magazine?"

Ruth picked up the magazine and pointed at the headline.

"Darling, the headline says it all."

"I don't understand."

"It's simple."

Ruth opened the magazine to the page where there was a full page picture of her on the set of *From The Big Apple* along with the article about her. She handed the magazine to William. He took it, looked at it and then looked at Ruth. She looked back at William. "Sit down. Why don't you read the article aloud to me? I will help you with the words you don't understand."

William sat down and started to read.

"Ruth Newcomb, former host of the syn-d—" William paused turning his head sideways as he tried to pronounce the word.

"Syndicated," Ruth finished.

"--syn-di-cated television show *From the Big Apple*, was born in East Hampton, New York. The so—" William paused again.

"Socialite," again Ruth finished the word for William.

Ruth and William were so involved, Ruth didn't notice the wild turkey, chickens, and néné had made their way to the porch and started eating Mrs. Wiggins' food.

"The so-cial-ite attended St. Francis Academy for girls and graduated mag-na co-me la-" William paused.

"That's magna cum laude, it's Latin meaning ..."

The sound of the birds pecking drew Ruth's attention. She looked at the birds, got up and chased them away. "Shoo, shoo!"

William started to laugh.

"Darling, what's so funny? Every day they come, every day the same thing."

"Why don't you give dem food, too?"

"That's Mrs. Wiggins' food. I don't want to feed the entire island!"

"Da birds, dey eat bugs. Dey good for you."

"I'm not going to feed them and that's final!"

✱ ✱ ✱

Ruth collected her mail from her post office box while Danny, the local television producer, was collecting his.

"Excuse me, aren't you Ruth Newcomb?"

"Yes, Darling, who else would I be?"

"Aaa-loooo-haa! I'm Danny Mauka, station manager at KBI, Big Island TV, channel 32."

Ruth acknowledged Danny. "Nice to meet you."

"I'm sure you have made quite a few adjustments to life here on da Big Island."

"Darling, more than you would ever want to know."

"Da first few months are tough and you'll adjust."

Ruth closed her mailbox as Danny continued, "Would you be interested in doing a broadcast or two?"

"Darling, I am not interested in doing television, radio, or anything right now. I just want to be left alone."

Danny reached into his pocket and pulled out a business card and handed it to Ruth.

"Here's my card. If you change your mind call me."

* * *

Ruth wore slacks for the first time along with a large hat covering her face from the sun, was kneeling in the garden clipping flowers and placed them in a Tiffany ceramic basin at her side. Mrs. Wiggins was curled up next to her. William was seated in an Adirondack chair reading an article from *The New Yorker*. He placed the magazine on the table, looked up at Ruth, "I finished, Mrs. Newcomb."

Ruth put the clipping sheers down, got up and took her seat in the Adirondack chair next to William.

"Excellent, William." William smiled. "You have made a significant improvement in your reading."

"It's coming a lot easier, thanks to you and Auntie."

On the table was a new paperback edition of *The Adventures of Huckleberry Finn*. Ruth reached for the paperback.

"I think reading is an adventure and it's about time you start reading a novel. We'll start out with an easy and fun one, *The Adventures of Huckleberry Finn*." Ruth handed the paperback to William and he started to flip through the book.

"What type of name is Huckleberry? Is he related to Huckleberry Hound, the cartoon dog?"

"No, but that's not important. What is important is that you enjoy Huck's adventures."

"Huck?"

"Darling, that's short for Huckleberry. You will get into the story and won't be able to put the book down."

"Ma-ha-lo, Mrs. Newcomb."

William opened the book, flipped to chapter one, and started to read. After a moment, he looked up, "It says he was in another book called *The Adventures of Tom Sawyer*. Should I read that book first?"

"I think this book is better."

"Oh-kay, but he sure writes funny."

"That's known as colloquial writing." Ruth noticed William cocked his head and continued, "Colloquial is like Auntie, when she speaks, that is known as Hawaiian Pidgin. In the case with the book, that is how Huck speaks. It will take you no time to pick it up. Continue reading, William."

William started reading. His lips slightly moved with each word as though he was reading aloud. Ruth watched William.

* * *

Ruth was watching television. Mrs. Wiggins was curled up on her lap. Ben entered through the front door.

"Good evening, Mrs. Newcomb."

"Good evening." After a brief moment, she asked, "Darling, have you found a security system yet?"

"No."

"I want you to check on it in the morning, okay?"

"Oh-kay."

* * *

The night was still. Ruth was sleeping, wearing her silk night mask. The grunting and popping sounds were so loud they awakened Ruth. She removed her night mask and sat on the edge of the bed. Mrs. Wiggins waddled into the bedroom meowing. Ruth reached into the night stand, took out a large flashlight, and turned it on as she headed outside.

Ruth used the flashlight to guide her; making her way towards the grunting and popping sounds. She turned the flashlight toward the sounds, which illuminated a large one hundred and fifty pound feral pig, grunting and scratching the ground near the base of a macadamia tree eating the nuts. The macadamia shells were so hard that when the pig bit down and broke the shell, it sounded like gun fire. Distracted by the light, the pig looked at Ruth, grunted, snorted, and waddled away into the darkness.

NO MORE KEIKI'S

A bright sunlight filtered through the mango and other fruit trees that border the macadamia orchard. Ruth checked the mango fruit to see if it was ready to eat before she continued walking through the orchard. She looked down at the ankle high grass, frowned and shook her head in disgust, as she saw a plethora of macadamia nuts on the ground. Under a few trees were large sized holes where the grass had been dug up by the night visitors. Ruth was getting mad. She looked around for Ben. Not seeing him nearby, she called, "Ben!" After a few moments, she called, "Ben!" Ruth walked faster, past her house and headed up to Auntie's, calling, "Ben!" She passed through the trees and shrubs that separated her property from Auntie's. She found the greenhouse and headed for it. She called, "Ben! Are you in there, Ben?"

"Uh-huh!" Ben replied.

Ruth opened the door to the greenhouse and was greeted with the aroma of skunk and grass. She entered and found Ben and Auntie clipping marijuana buds from mature plants. They both looked up at Ruth.

"You, kokua?" Auntie inquired.

"No, I came for Ben."

Ruth took a moment and looked around the greenhouse. Her jaw dropped as she realized the keiki's were not at all kids or little ones, but marijuana plants.

"That's marijuana!" She exclaimed.

"Haole call it marijuana, we call it pakalolo. You kokua?" Auntie responded.

Ruth did not like the current arrangement one bit. "What you are doing here is wrong. Ben, I want you down at my place, now!"

Ben put his head down as if he was caught in the act of doing something terribly wrong, "Oh-kay."

Ruth turned to leave.

"No!" Auntie commanded "Ben stay. Keiki's need kokua, now!"

"No! Darling, Ben will come with me, to my place. I pay him to take care of my place."

"I pay Ben, too. Da pakalolo help people and make more money den mac nuts, Kona coffee, and orchids."

"What you all are doing is wrong; growing marijuana is illegal."

"Dis is medicinal marijuana." Auntie clarified.

"I don't care." Ruth said then looked at Ben, "Ben, come!"

Ben shook his head.

"Ben," Ruth continued, "you were hired to take care of my place. You haven't mowed the lawn in over a month. The nuts need attention and the security system. Well, what about the security system?"

"I work it."

"Enough of this, Ben, I have had all I can take of you and your lack of work. If you like it so much here, Ben, get your stuff out of my place and move up here with Auntie."

Auntie glared at Ruth, "He no live wit me."

"I want Ben out of my place tomorrow. You understand?"

✳ ✳ ✳

On the lanai, Ruth typed on her laptop. Mrs. Wiggins was curled up in her usual sunny spot. William approached carrying *The Adventures of Huckleberry Finn*. Smiling as he reached Ruth, "Aaa-loooo-haa, Mrs. Newcomb... Am I disturbing you?"

"No, Darling. Have a seat." William took his seat in the other Adirondack chair.

"You were right, Mrs. Newcomb. I couldn't put *Huck Finn* down. It is a great book! I could really identify with Huck cause we have a lot in common. I really liked the part where he uses pigs blood to fake his death."

"It was a great story, wasn't it?"

"Yes, Mrs. Newcomb. Ma-ha-lo!"

William returned the book to Ruth, who placed it on the table next to *Catcher in the Rye*, which she handed to William commenting, "You know, William, *Catcher in the Rye* is a great book. You will like it too."

"Ma-ha-lo!"

"William, I need help around the house, mow the lawn, collect the nuts, and do odd jobs. Do you know of anyone?"

"Ben, he da bomb. There is no one betta than Ben."

"So you don't know of anyone?" Ruth asked.

William shook his head no.

"Darling, would you help me?"

"I am not Ben. I do not have tools or experience like him." William responded as started to get up. "I need to go help Auntie."

"Why are you helping her with that stuff? You shouldn't engage in such activities."

William sat back down, "That stuff? Such activities? I don't understand."

"You know what I mean, William."

"No, I don't, Mrs. Newcomb!"

"What you are doing is wrong."

85

"There is nothing wrong with helping Auntie."

"William, I agree with you to a point. However, helping someone tend marijuana is not."

"Helping ohana is da Hawaiian way."

"If you go up there and help her with that stuff, I don't want you around here anymore."

William got up and said, "What-ever..." as he started up the hill, still holding *Catcher in the Rye*.

BE CAREFUL WHAT YOU WISH FOR

It was a peaceful night until the sounds of the crickets and frogs were abruptly interrupted by the sounds of Mrs. Wiggins outside in a cat fight along with grunting sounds awakened Ruth. She removed the night mask, got out of bed calling, "Mrs. Wiggins! Mrs. Wiggins!"

Ruth, with flashlight in hand, ran frantically into the orchard toward the sounds of Mrs. Wiggins hissing and the pig grunting. Ruth reached the scene, shining her flashlight on the pig, only to watch it meander away, leaving Mrs. Wiggins sprawled on the grass.

"Mrs. Wiggins!" Ruth stopped dead in her tracks not believing the carnage in front of her. "Oh, no, Mrs. Wiggins!"

* * *

A light rain fell as Ruth finished digging a hole in the soft red volcanic soil to bury her beloved cat. Ruth reached down taking Mrs. Wiggins, who was wrapped in

Ruth's New York red woolen scarf, looking like a mummy. She ceremoniously placed the cat in the hole and filled it with soil and placed a handmade wooden cross at end of the makeshift grave and said a silent prayer. Ruth stood and shook her head in disbelief. She looked towards the house, the orchard, and the ocean realizing the vastness and loneliness of the island and started to cry.

* * *

Later, Ruth sat on her lanai with the open laptop, staring pensively at the screen and shook her head. She closed the laptop, got up, walked down the steps of the lanai to the garden area where Mrs. Wiggins was buried, looked at the barren burial site, and sorrowfully shook her head.

Unnoticed by Ruth, Auntie quietly walked up; placed her hands together in front of her and bowed her head. After a few moments, Auntie started to speak. However, this time in perfect American scholastic English with no accent.

"It's hard when we lose loved ones, isn't it?"

Startled, Ruth turned and looked at her.

"It will take time," Auntie continued, "and you will get over it. You need a hug..." Auntie opened her arms to Ruth. "Come to Auntie."

Ruth hesitated.

"It's oh-kay," encouraged Auntie, "I am here for you."

Ruth hesitantly raised her hands to hug Auntie.

"You need someone right now. Auntie's here."

Ruth finally could not resist. The two of them embraced in a hug. Ruth started to cry.

"There, there." Auntie patted Ruth as though she were consoling a frightened child. "Everything is going to be alright."

Ruth sobbed, "Mrs. Wiggins was the last thing I had. I wanted to be alone, but not like this."

After a few moments, Ruth and Auntie broke their embrace. Auntie looked at Ruth, "Sometimes, what we want is not what we truly need. Oftentimes, what we are looking for is right in front of us and we don't see it. We look elsewhere because we believe it is there and not where it truly is. You came from the fast paced, wikiwiki, world of the Big Apple, to the more relaxed laid back life of the Big Island. The two cannot coexist. You are here now, but for how long?"

Ruth shrugged her shoulders. "I sold everything and am here for good."

"You're a multi-millionaire. You can move back to the Big Apple anytime you want."

"There's nothing left for me there."

"Then you must adjust to the Big Island life. Here, we help each other, we are all one big family, it's the Hawaiian way. The Hawaiians call it ohana. Ohana is the Hawaiian word for family, it doesn't only mean our blood family, it also means our extended family; the family that is there for us in the here and now. William is not my son, but I treat him as though he is. That's ohana. Hawaii was built on ohana; it is the magic of the Hawaiian people."

Ruth thought for a moment or two, "I think I understand. My needs and wants are out of whack, they are not set for the Hawaiian way, they are currently set for the Big Apple. That's in the past. I need to move on, as Mrs. Strong said when she arrived from the mainland, she used to be uptight and that life is different here and she changed; she said, in time, I too would change and become more relaxed and enjoy da Big Island ways."

Auntie looked towards her house and back at Ruth.

"Would you like to have punch?"

"I'd love to."

Ruth and Auntie walked through the orchard towards Auntie's house.

"You are speaking perfect English now. So why do you speak pidgin?"

"It's expected!" Auntie smiled, "I have my Ph.D. in horticulture from Purdue and if I were to speak proper English, things would be completely different. Besides, I enjoy speaking pidgin. Very few people know I have my doctorate, I keep that and speaking perfect English to a select group who have at least a master's degree, like the Baccio's, Charlene, and Dr. Tilton; other than them, people think I'm that sweet crazy Auntie born and raised on Oahu. In due time, you'll be speaking pidgin too."

* * *

Ruth was still over dressed, wearing a designer outfit, while Auntie, a missionary dress, as they walked into Macy's. Auntie was speaking perfect English with Ruth, "We need to change your mainland attire to that of a kama'aina."

"A what?" Ruth asked.

"Kama'aina is the Hawaiian for child of the land or better known as a local person. Haole used to mean white person, but now, to be politically correct, it means foreigner. This is all part of what I have been talking about, changing your mindset to be a part of da Big Island." Auntie lowered her voice and continued "We have a secret."

Ruth leaned into Auntie as not to miss a word.

"As I told you the other day, you know something very few other people do."

"Darling, what could I possibly know that no one else knows?"

"My education and use of pidgin! It's between us girls. From now on, I will only speak pidgin. And you must cut that darling stuff. Using darling may work in the Big Apple, but not here on da Big Island. We do things differently here." Auntie leaned even closer into Ruth and winks. "You understand, sista?"

Ruth laughed as they entered Macy's.

* * *

Ruth exited Macy's wearing, for the first time, a muumuu and zoris, carrying a few bags. Next stop was Lowe's where both were pushing their carts into the garden department. Ruth looked at an assortment of smaller potted plants, picked up the more vivacious flowers, smelling them, before placing them in her cart. When she was done, Ruth joined Auntie who was putting two bags of fertilizer into her cart. As Ruth approached Auntie patted the fertilizer saying, "Dis kokua, da keiki's."

"I don't understand why you are growing that stuff."

Auntie leaned close to Ruth whispering in perfect English, "It's one way I can afford to live here."

"So you see nothing wrong with what you are doing?"

"There is nothing wrong with it. It's not like I'm trafficking or selling to kids."

"So that makes it okay?"

"Yes, I'm registered with the feds on an experimental horticultural program doing research on growing medicinal marijuana which we hope sometime in the future will help a lot of suffering people." Auntie continued, "Did you know cannabis cures certain types of cancer? The Chinese have been using it for thousands of years. Cannabis is in its infancy. With more research it will be the wonder drug."

"So, why does Ben spend so much time with you?"

"He normally doesn't, it's harvest time and I can use all the help I can get. You're welcome to help any time."

Auntie moved back from Ruth continuing in pidgin. "It da Hawaiian way!"

Ruth spotted chicken feed and grabbed a twenty-five pound bag and added it to her cart.

A NEW LIFE BEGINS

After Ruth got home she took the flowers to Mrs. Wiggins' grave site and carefully planted them in a colorful arrangement around the burial mound to ensure they marked the exact location where Mrs. Wiggins was enjoying eternity.

Afterwards, she stood admiring her diligent work at making a beautiful tropical memorial for Mrs. Wiggins. She reminisced the first time she was introduced to Mrs. Wiggins when Carol Burnett and Tim Conway made an appearance on *From the Big Apple*. Carol presented the kitten to Ruth and named it after her *Carol Burnett Show* character Mrs. Wiggins, the secretary to Mr. Tudball, played by Tim Conway. Whenever Carol or Tim appeared on *From the Big Apple*, Ruth made sure Mrs. Wiggins made an appearance, she knew Carol, Tim, and her audience loved the Mrs. Wiggins updates on the cats growth and antics.

When Ruth returned to the house, she saw a plethora of birds pecking the ground. She went up the stairs of the lanai into the kitchen to prepare the chicken feed. She filled Mrs. Wiggins bowl with the remaining cat food, then chicken feed, mixing them together before returning to the base of the lanai steps, placing the bowl on the first step. She decided the first step was best because the birds would not otherwise see the cat bowl due to the long thick grass that would obscure the bowl. Ruth turned to go back up the stairs into the house, when she reached the door, loud cackling was heard from the base of the lanai. She turned to see three chickens pecking the feed in the bowl. Nearby, a rooster started crowing which started to attract other chickens and birds. In the distance, she heard the gobbling of the wild turkeys as they too, heard the commotion and made their way to the foot of the lanai. Ruth proud of her accomplishment of taking the first small step of being one with nature and more Hawaiian like and smiled.

The following day, Ruth wearing jeans, T-shirt, and zoris was inside the shed which housed the lawn mowing tractor. She climbed onto the seat of the tractor and was able to locate the on/off switch, other switches, including the one that operated the mowing blades. She set the blades in the off position and started the tractor. The tractor sound was a little louder than she had expected, but felt she could quickly adjust to the sound. Ruth felt like she did when she was a child in a rumble seat; vibrating and shaking her even though she wasn't moving. She looked down at the floorboard and saw pedals. With a little trepidation, she pressed the gas pedal. The tractor lurched forward so abruptly, she almost fell off and barely missed taking out part of the shed as she did. Realizing the pedal was overly sensitive Ruth gently pressed it and cautiously pulled out of the shed.

Ruth felt it best to head directly to the orchard where she could learn how to use the lawn tractor before doing the areas nearer her house. On the way to the orchard, she felt she could also learn how to cut the grass before getting to the orchard and engaged the mower. At first, she wasn't doing a good job, she could not drive straight nor control the mower. As she drove, the chickens, wild turkey, and néné scurried out of her way. Ruth knew she would master the mower with time and practiced making turns in the open grassy area before reaching the orchard. With each turn, she did better at mastering the nuances of mower. Before entering the orchard, she paused for a moment to look at her work to see the crooked lane of cut grass which lead from the shed. The smell of fresh cut grass permeated the air. The birds had returned to the freshly cut lane pecking and eating fresh grubs and bugs the mower had kicked up.

Looking at the macadamia trees in the orchard, she realized she would have to be very careful as not to hit her head and navigate around the lower hanging branches. After a few hours, Ruth had finished cutting the grass in the orchard and around the house. The entire time, the birds followed behind the mower enjoying the fruits of her labor. Near the shed was a large mango tree with oversized hanging fruit too high to reach from the ground. There no was reason to mow around the tree, since grass wasn't growing there. Ruth thought the ripe mangos would make a great meal. With the mower disengaged, she drove the tractor to the edge of the tree, reached up and picked two large ripe mangos before expertly navigating the tractor into the shed.

NEW YORK CANNOT BE ALL THAT BAD

On the lanai, Ruth typed on her laptop, as William approached.

"Mrs. Newcomb, here's *Catcher in the Rye*."

William handed her the book and started to leave. Ruth placed the book on the table.

"William, please come back."

William returned, still standing.

"William, I want to apologize for my rudeness the other day. It was wrong of me."

"Dat oh-kay, Mrs. Newcomb. Ben's brother, Michael, lives in New York, he says New Yorker's can be very rude."

"We New Yorkers really are not rude, William, but sometimes the customs and the way of life of other cultures, even our own here in the United States, are misunderstood and taken as being rude or unacceptable."

"I think I understand. Do you have another fun book?"

Ruth thought for a moment, and then snapped her fingers. "Come with me, William." William followed Ruth to the book shelf in the living room. She scanned the book shelf. "Ah, here it is."

Ruth reached for James Michener's *Hawaii* and handed the book to William. William looked at the thick book; his eyes widened in amazement.

"The book is soooo thick."

"William, it's a good read. You will enjoy it."

William took the book, "Thank you, Mrs. Newcomb. I am sure I will like it as I did the other books." William started to leave. "Auntie's keiki's need me."

"Mind if I tag along?"

William looked at Ruth and shook his head no. Ruth closed the laptop and placed it on the table next to the chair. Leaving the laptop out in the open for all to see is something she would never do in New York. She slipped on her zoris and got up.

Ruth and William walked together through the orchard headed for Auntie's. William curiously asked, "I thought you didn't like what we are doing and now you want to help?"

"William, let's say I need to adjust from my New York ways and customs to those here on the Big Island."

"That brings up a question. Is New York as wicked and phony as Holden Caulfield says it is?" William asked.

"From Holden's perspective it is. From mine, New York isn't really that way."

"I didn't think so, because you aren't like the people in the book."

"I don't know if I should take that as a compliment or not."

"Oh, a compliment, Mrs. Newcomb. I couldn't put da book down. Reading is fun, just like you, Auntie, Mrs. Strong, and Dr. Tilton told me. I discovered so much about New York."

"Just think about it, William, you were able to accomplish it without leaving the island. And now you will discover Hawaii. It's a fictional account of Hawaii, and it is fairly accurate to what happened and how the islands became the way they are."

They reached Auntie's greenhouse. William entered followed by Ruth. Auntie and Ben, harvesting buds, looked up. Ruth looked apologetically at Ben whom she had not seen since she banished him.

"Ben, I want to apologize about my behavior the *da* other day."

This was the first time Ruth had used the word *da* for *the*. Both Ben and Auntie noticed the change and reacted by smiling. Ruth continued to address Ben, "You can come back."

"Mahalo," Ben pausing a moment before continuing, "I thought you didn't like what we are doing here."

"I've been thinking, helping each other is da Hawaiian way, isn't it? I'm here to help." Ruth caught herself continuing, "Ah, I mean I am here to kokua."

"You go, sista!" Auntie proclaimed.

Auntie saw William was carrying *Hawaii*. She looked at William, "Dat good book! It Hawaii to da max."

"It is a *big* book."

"You read. You like. Yes?"

William nodded. "Mrs. Newcomb said I would like it, too."

Ruth saw Auntie and Ben had buckets and shears.

"Where do I get a bucket?"

Ben leaned into Auntie, "She never done dis before."

"What can be so hard about trimming?" Ruth responded.

"There's a special way, I'll show you." Ben offered.

"No," Auntie exclaimed, "she learn from da masta. I show her! Come."

Ruth walked towards Auntie. William placed *Hawaii* on the counter, picked up a small bucket and shears, and started harvesting buds, while Auntie showed Ruth how to harvest and placed the fresh cuttings in the bucket.

"See, it not hard. You try."

Ruth followed the same procedure shown to her by Auntie.

"You do plenny good. You get bucket."

* * *

Later that afternoon, Ruth was on her lanai typing on her laptop. Ben walked up the steps carrying a large UPS cardboard box. He had his tool belt on and asked, "Mrs. Newcomb, what do you want done first?"

Ruth stopped typing, looking up, "What are you talking about, Ben?"

"You asked for a security system, I got da system. It's here in da box. Do you want da front door or your bedroom done first?"

"Ben, I no longer need a security system."

"Since you got here, you wanted a security system, now you don't?" Ben confirmed.

"*Dis* is Hawaii. You said Hawaii is laid-back. No one has a security system. We don't need it. Give it to me, I'll return it."

OH, DEM PIGS!

For almost a week, the sounds of the rain hitting the metal roof followed by the sounds of the insects chirping and frogs croaking lulled Ruth to sleep; she no longer needed her silk night mask. However, one particular evening the enjoyable sounds of the rain forest were abruptly broken by the nearby grunting and popping sounds of a pig. Ruth reached into her nightstand and grabbed the flashlight and headed out into the darkness to locate the pig. The sounds were coming from Mrs. Wiggins' gravesite and nearby mango tree. Ruth pointed the flashlight towards the gravesite and saw the flowers were gone, apparently eaten by the pig. Hearing a loud thud followed by a grunt, she pointed the flashlight towards the mango tree and saw the pig ramming the trunk with its body as a ripe mango fell to the ground. The light attracted the attention of the pig who looked at her as it ate the mango and trotted away into the darkness.

The following morning, Ruth and Auntie were on Auntie's lanai having coffee. It was just the two of them, so Auntie was speaking in perfect English.

"The pigs are a major issue on the island and need to be kept in check. It's especially hard to do where we live because our properties are near a state park where the pigs are protected. I believe the pigs figured out that they are safe and cavort there.

"Usually fences do a great job of keeping the pigs out, I've been thinking that once harvesting is over, we have Ben put up fences around our properties. My concern is they may get to the pakalolo. Can you imagine what would happen with a pig high on marijuana?"

Ruth nodded with laughter. "What do we do to keep them out?"

"Keeping the fences in check is our first line of defense. Right now we have to have Ben trap and dispatch them."

"Dispatch them?" Ruth inquired.

"Kill them, donating their carcasses to needy families, a local luau, or someone who would love fresh pork. For the other undesirables, such as mongoose, Ben dispatches them to what we locals call another zip code; meaning a field a few miles from here so they don't return. Having Ben around is such a help for us women.

"Paul once shot a 200 pound pig. A few days later, the Martin's had Ben prep and cook da pig in their Imu, that's the large earthen barbecue pit near your shed, and had a luau for their friends and ohana before they returned to New York."

"I remember them telling us about that adventure. They said the pig was tender and succulent."

"The rifle should still be somewhere in your house."

"It's in my closet." Ruth added. "Are you suggesting I shoot the pig?"

"Oh, not at all. There may be a night where you may need to protect yourself from da pigs, they sometimes get aggressive and may charge you. When they charge you, you have two choices either climb a tree or shoot. When I hear them at night, I always take my rifle. Luckily the flashlight usually scares them and they trot away. Like what happened to you last night."

"I have at least two mongoose running around my place. I thought they would be like the squirrels in Central Park looking for a hand out. They run away from me when I approach them. They don't seem to be an issue. So why would Ben dispatch them?" Ruth queried.

"Mongoose aren't really an issue, they love to consume eggs. With all the chickens around we have a plethora of fresh eggs. Wait here!"

Auntie left Ruth on the lanai and returned moments later carrying a bowl with two eggs, one of which was slightly smaller than the other. Auntie took both eggs out of the bowl and placed the bowl and both eggs next to their coffee mugs. She pointed to the smaller egg.

"This egg is from one of the feral chickens. See how it's slightly smaller than the store bought egg." Auntie took the larger egg into her hand and cracked it open into the bowl and followed doing the same thing with the smaller egg and handed the bowl for Ruth to inspect.

"Notice the difference in the yokes?"

"The yoke from the smaller egg is much larger than the store bought egg. Why is it?" Ruth asked.

"It means the egg is feral, on the mainland they like to use phrases like organic or free range eggs. You probably haven't seen any eggs because your mongoose are eating the eggs before you know they are there. We'll have Ben dispatch the mongoose to another zip code. Most of all, the feral eggs are free and much more tastier than the store bought ones. Would you like scrambled eggs for breakfast?"

RUTH'S IDEA

Ruth drove down the road towards Waipio Valley past the Honoka'a Post Office and Mr. Woo's where she saw three tall palm trees that formed the letters TV below which was a modern yet rustic looking wooden sign with green lettering identifying the metal Quonset hut as being KBI-TV, Big Island TV, Channel 32. Ruth parked and entered.

The austerity of the interior bore a strange resemblance to Captain Binghamton's office from the 1960's *McHale's Navy* television series. Behind the sole desk in the front reception area of the hut was a young twenties something Hawaiian woman, playing solitaire on the computer, looked up at Ruth as she entered the building.

"May I help you?"

"Yes, I'm Ruth Newcomb and am here to see Danny."

"He's expecting you. Go ahead and enter."

"Thank you."

Ruth entered Danny's office to find him typing on the computer, he looked up and stood as she entered. The office looked as though it was frozen in time with the television playing a re-run of *Gilligan's Island*.

"Come in." Danny pointed to one of the two chairs in front of his desk. "Have a seat. Good to finally officially meet you. May I call you Ruth?"

"Yes, of course, darling, er, Danny."

"I was hoping you would call." Danny continued. "I like your idea for a Big Island travelogue series."

"I do have one request." Ruth asked. "Alexander Mackendrick, director of *Sweet Smell of Success* and dean of California Institute of the Arts Film School kept an egg timer on his desk. When students would pitch an idea, he told them, 'If you cannot finish your pitch by the time the egg timer runs out, don't come back until you can.' And turned the egg timer upside down. I thought we could utilize the same concept with our segments, keep them as short as we can while getting the true essence across."

"What an unusual yet creative idea. I don't see an issue with keeping the segments short." Danny hesitated a moment before continuing, "Ruth, you do realize we can't pay you what you got in New York."

"That's okay. This is Hawaii, things are different here. I want da money to go to da Honokaa Library. They need it more than I do."

"What a wonderful thing to do for the island."

Ruth smiled. "Ma-ha-lo, Danny."

"If the show is anything like *From the Big Apple* both locals and tourists will like it." Danny continued, "What do you think about calling da show *From the Big Island?*"

"Love it! However, *From the Big Island* doesn't sound just right." Ruth responded.

"I think it's perfect."

"Well, it is almost perfect. What I was thinking is we need to make a minor change," Danny cocked his head as Ruth continued, "making it more Hawaiian and change the word *the* to *da*. It's da Hawaiian way, correct?"

Danny raised his eyebrows, smiled and nodded, "I love it!"

"It will make all da difference. We'll call it *From da Big Island.* However, we need something else."

"Like what?" Danny inquired.

"When I did *From the Big Apple*, our logo was a large stylized apple behind da title. We need to do something similar, perhaps a palm tree?"

"Over done."

"Hibiscus flower?"

"Over done."

"A lotus flower."

"Over done."

Danny stared into space for a moment and then snapped his fingers. "I got it!"

"What?"

"FBI!"

"FBI?" Ruth responded.

"Yes, *FBI - From da Big Island.* Get it?"

Ruth nodded.

Danny continued, "We have FBI in large yellow letters, with *From da Big Island* in a smaller font."

"Won't people get confused with *the* FBI?"

"I don't think so, this is Hawaii, not da mainland. We'll even put the da in small letters between the F and B. How could anyone misinterpret that logo between us and the Federal Bureau of Investigation?"

Ruth cracked a smile, "We still may have legal issues. And there are other big islands around the world. We need to better identify our Big Island of Hawaii from other big islands.

"When we came up with da logo for *From the Big Apple*, we put the name of da show inside a line drawing of an apple. What if we did something similar, such as encapsulating da letters FBI inside an outline of the island? That way we have something unique, thereby reducing any confusion."

"What a wonderful idea, Ruth." Danny exclaimed, nodding in agreement, continued, "Have you given much thought as to what you would like to do for your first installment?"

"I was thinking of doing something on Waipio Valley."

"I don't think that would be a good idea. It's been overdone and on da tourist channel."

"Yes, but not my angle."

Ruth wore a missionary dress and a red hibiscus behind her left ear looking directly into the television camera, "Many tourists and locals alike attempt to drive the arduous journey down the Waipio Valley access road and just don't quite make it; plunging two to three-hundred feet to the valley floor." She turned, looked up, and pointed towards a couple of rusted car carcasses resting in the trees. After a moment, "Okay, let's get the cutaway shots of da cars."

Mickey, the cameraman, swung the video camera upwards pointing it towards the cars in trees.

"Mickey," Danny added "don't forget to include the ones where the trees have grown around and through the cars." Mickey took the camera and walked into the brush to get cutaway shots of the rusted cars in the trees.

Danny walked up to Ruth, "This is a great idea of yours, Ruth. It's unique."

"Thank you, Danny. I thought everyone knows about da cars, but no one talks about them."

"Yeah, I remember six month ago, about the same time you arrived on the island, when a couple of drunk tourist kids, thought they would drive their rental car down here to party on da beach. They almost made it. Da only thing that saved them from being killed was da tree. They were so drunk they didn't feel a thing. When they awoke the next morning, they realized how lucky they were."

"Do you know where their car is?"

Danny looked up in the trees searching for the car. "It's here somewhere." Danny continued searching the trees. "I really can't remember exactly where it is. You can tell which one it is because the car isn't as rusted as da others and it was a convertible."

* * *

Ruth, Ben, and Auntie were all drinking red punch and eating brownies watching Ruth's television set on which was Ruth ending her Waipio car segment. "That's it from the Waipio Valley graveyard of cars in the trees. Until next time, this is Ruth Newcomb, *From da Big Island.* Aaa-looo-haaa!" The credits rolled by.

"Dat gut!" Auntie exclaimed as she looked at Ruth.

"It funny, too," Ben added.

Ruth is beaming. "Mahalo!"

"Der you go. You become mo like Hawaiian." Auntie told Ruth as she took a bite from a brownie.

"Auntie, the punch and brownies are fabulous!" Ruth exclaimed, "Whatever do you put in them?"

"Coconut water make da punch." Auntie responded.

"Da brownies are from an old Hawaiian family recipe." Ben added.

TIME FLIES

Ruth drove down Alii Drive towards the Royal Kona Hotel, which looked like a stylized volcano across Kailua Bay. She was excited because she was picking up her first visitor since she moved to the island. She drove into the front entrance of the hotel, where Gloria La Fong was waiting for her. She stopped and got out.

"Gloria, Aaa-looo-haa!" Ruth said as they embraced.

"Aloha! You look fantastic. I can't wait to hear about what is going on."

"I'll tell you all about it, Gloria. I thought we'd have lunch at a little restaurant I know that has the best seafood on the island. The only thing is, it doesn't have a waterfront view. Would that be okay?"

"You know the island best, Ruth. You always go to the best places."

* * *

They entered the Big Island Grill, which looked like a converted fast food restaurant. On a wall inside was a poster displaying a plethora of fish with both their Hawaiian and mainland names and next to it a chalk board written with *Fresh Fish Today – Opah and Hapu'upu'u*. Both Ruth and Gloria were not sure what Hapu'upu'u or Opah were, they studied the chart finding that Hapu'upu'u was grouper and Opah was moonfish.

"Ruth, have you been to a hukilau yet?"

"Not yet. I think it's a wonderful idea to shoot a real hukilau from throwing out the hukilau nets, to the beach festival and dance that follows."

"I'm sure you could integrate the hukilau song in the segment."

"Gloria, you are filled with ideas."

* * *

Seated and eating their lunch, "Ruth, you've been avoiding telling me how are you are adjusting. How are you really doing?"

"Gloria, remember how a wreck I was after Zach's death?" Gloria nodded as Ruth continued. "I thought his death was hard on me, but worse, was the way I lost Mrs. Wiggins to that damned pig. What a way for her to go. It still makes me mad when I think about it. They are becoming a major issue here on the island. We did a segment on *From da Big Island* about the pig issue. It was well received, but there is nothing we can do to reduce the population explosion. Ben has been making extra money dispatching pigs."

"Dispatching? I don't understand." Gloria inquired.

"Killing and selling them for luau's or donating them to families in need."

"What a great thing for him to do, taking care of those in need. Do the pigs taste any different than what we get in the states?"

"Gloria, Hawaii is a state. It's best to say mainland. However, to answer your question, I haven't had any yet. I understand there is nothing better in the world than a pig cooked the Hawaiian way in an Imu, a Hawaiian underground oven, for the entire day. I have one by the shed and hope to use it."

"You still are avoiding answering my question on how are you doing."

"Gloria, I prefer to spend our time together not as your patient, but as a friend. In that respect, things are going great, I am keeping busy with *From da Big Island*, writing my memoirs, and helping a local high school senior with his reading."

* * *

Ruth and Danny were seated together at his office desk reviewing legal papers. "Ruth, I think I have everything in order. Da two of us are da executive producers. Partial funding comes from da visitors bureau and our head offices in New York."

"Danny, did they put it in writing?"

"Ruth, it's right here." Danny took the contract and handed it to Ruth with his finger resting on the middle of the page. "See? *From da Big Island.*"

Ruth looked at the contract. "I was afraid with da show going into syndication New York would want to change da name to *From the Big Island.*"

"They loved it and agreed to partner with da visitors bureau to develop an advertising campaign. Da logo will go on T-shirts, coffee mugs, and the like. They're going all out." Ruth smiled as Danny continued, "Since you did a great job conveying so much information about da Big Island in so little time, everyone agreed to keep to the original short format. Da visitors bureau can utilize our segments as public service announcements throughout the world."

"That is wonderful news, Danny. We've come a long way in a short time. Our segments have been very popular from our first one with cars in da trees segment to da one we did on da sports fishers throwing chum into the water drawing da sharks that were attacking da swimmers."

"And, we cannot forget da pigs!" Danny added, "The way you set everyone up with da pig issue. Dat scene where da pigs were eating da ears of corn, then cutting to da pig at da luau with da ears of corn strategically placed around da pig was precious." They both laughed.

"Danny, I was so busy filming that pig segment, I didn't have a chance to enjoy the event. One of these days, I will."

* * *

Joe and Eileen Baccio decided to make a layover in the Hawaiian Islands on their return trip from Southeast Asia. They visited the Martin's numerous times over the years, know their neighbors, and loved the Big Island. It was Joe's idea to invite both Ruth and Auntie to the Mauna Kea Hotel Clam Bake Saturday evening.

The four of them sat beachside, where an elaborate buffet feast of fresh island lobster, fish, sushi, sashimi, prime rib, and other wonderful food.

Auntie spoke perfect English, as she generally did when she was alone with the Martin's, Baccio's, and Ruth. Auntie brought Joe up to date with the advancements she was making with her medicinal marijuana project and how she was developing a much more powerful strain that she knew would help the millions in need.

"What we need to see happen," Auntie continued, "is changes in the law to make medicinal marijuana available nationwide. It's a shame to totally exclude something that can cure ailments, such as certain cancers, allow AIDS and HIV patients to eat, where they couldn't before. I think we're heading in the right direction."

"I couldn't agree with you more." Joe concurred. "Hopefully, one day the government will approve the medicinal use and people won't have to go underground to get their medications. Thank you for what you are doing and keep up the good work."

"To change the subject," Eileen said, "Joe and I are considering buying vacation property here."

"Buy here? It's so far from New York." Ruth replied.

"The Caribbean is just too crowded for us," Eileen continued, "as is Oahu. We prefer the more open and relaxed atmosphere of the Big Island. We don't like the rainforest side of the island where you both live. We prefer the dry side and are leaning towards Waikoloa Beach Resort area which has everything we need. Do you have any suggestions?"

"I haven't been here long enough to know what would work or not work for you, Joe." Ruth responded.

"Waikoloa Beach would be perfect for the both of you." Auntie add. "Like you said, it has everything you need and it doesn't get the rain like we do."

"When are you thinking on buying?" Ruth asked.

"Within the year." Joe responded.

"Ruth,." Eileen interjected. "I've noticed this is the first time we've been out and we haven't been interrupted with by your fans. I thought the show was very popular here."

"Eileen, the show is very popular. We're in the islands and people are different here. They respect my privacy. Every once in a while, some fans, generally from the mainland, will recognize and approach me for an autograph. What's nice is it doesn't happen all that frequently."

"We were watching TV last night and saw your segment on Queen Lili someone."

"Oh, you're talking about Queen Liliuokalani, the last Hawaiian monarch who was overthrown by the narrow-minded missionaries."

"It was a great informative segment."

"Eileen and I," Joe interrupted, "liked that she wanted to tax prostitution, the lottery, and opium because people were going to do it anyway and it was a revenue stream. I hope our government will also change its mind and tax medicinal marijuana like they did with the lottery. Only time will tell."

* * *

Ruth, Auntie, Ben, and William are all harvesting keiki's in Auntie's greenhouse. Their buckets were filled with buds. Auntie looked up at Ruth, "You do plenny good, Luka."

"Luka, what's that?"

William could not resist, "Dat Hawaiian for Ruth."

Ruth then remembered the Luka Newcomb sign Ben had at the airport when she arrived.

The door to the greenhouse opened as two police officers nonchalantly entered greeting everyone with "Aaa-loooo-haa!" Ruth's eyes widened as she looked towards Auntie.

"Aaa-looo-haaa!" Auntie, Ben, and William responded in unison.

Ruth was relieved, smiled, and added, "Aaa-loooo-haa!"

"Oh, Mrs. Newcomb," one of the officers addressed Ruth, "we want to congratulate you on your Emmy nomination."

"What are you talking about?" Ruth responded.

"It came over our radio that *From da Big Island* was nominated for an Emmy."

Everyone looked at Ruth and clapped.

"It was nominated for an Emmy!" Ruth exclaimed in astonishment. She had never thought *From da Big Island* was being considered for an Emmy.

"You go New York?" Auntie asked.

William looked at Ruth asking, "New York! Can I go with you?"

"With me, where?" Ruth responded.

"To New York!" William exclaimed.

"Dat's were da Emmy's are, aren't they?" Auntie added.

Ruth nodded, "Yes, they are in New York City." After a brief pause, Ruth continued, "I really don't want to return to New York."

"It is important, isn't it?" Ben asked.

"Oh, Luka, you must go." Auntie pleaded, "Dis is important to you, to us, and most of all, da Big Island."

DA BIG APPLE

Even though it was evening in New York City, the bright lights of the city illuminated the entrance of the Times Square Marriott Marquis Hotel as though it was still daylight. A black limo pulled into the valet area. The valet opened the limo door while a porter took the luggage out of the trunk. Danny stepped out, who turned around reached his hand into the limo and helped Ruth and Auntie out, all wore Aloha wear. Ruth, Auntie, and Danny stood and looked into the opened limo door. Moments later, Ruth leaned into the limo and said, "It's oh-kay. Come."

William stuck his head out the door looked at the valet and then focused his attention on the people briskly walking by "There are too many people!" William exclaimed, "Ben say he doesn't like all da people in New York. Dat's why he wouldn't come."

Ruth attempted to reassure William telling him, "Remember, Holden Caulfield in *Catcher in the Rye*. It's okay!"

Slowly William stepped out of the limo. A few people stared at the foursome next to the limo which was quite common in New York City, but what was uncommon was they wore Aloha wear.

"Are you from the tropics?" a porter inquired as he continued to place the luggage on the baggage cart.

"Yes, we're from Hawaii." Ruth responded before addressing her entourage. "We've had a very long flight, let's check in and get some rest before we explore the city."

"Can we see Times Square? Can we? Can we now, Mrs. Newcomb?"

"We'll explore tomorrow."

"Please?" William pleaded.

Auntie came to Williams' defense, "Da boy need to see Time Square at night. It unforgettable."

Ruth thought for a moment, then nodded, "Auntie's right. We'll go now." Ruth then addressed the porter, "Take these to check-in. We'll be back in a few minutes." The porter nodded. Ruth turned to the group, "Let's go, Times Square is right around the corner." William, Auntie, and Danny followed Ruth out of the Marquis entrance area into Times Square which was busy with cars and people rushing about. The lights of Times Square illuminated the groups awed faces.

"Here it is. This is Time Square."

William looked around the square, then up. "Da buildings are so tall; higher than the waterfall in Waipio."

"Remember the ball dropping in Times Square on New Year's eve?" Ruth asked the group; all nodded. "It happens over there." Ruth pointed towards One Times Square building.

People walked briskly by the foursome as they absorbed the Times Square commotion. Danny shook his head, "Too many people!"

Auntie added, "Dey too busy to enjoy life. Too, wikiwiki!"

"I don't think I like it here." William proclaimed.

"William, you just arrived. We are in the busiest area of New York. Central Park is not far from here and it isn't anything like this." Ruth exclaimed, in an attempt to quell William's first impression of New York.

"I'm tired. Can we go to our room?" William responded.

* * *

The bellhop held the door for Ruth, Auntie, William, and Danny as they entered the enormous Presidential Suite.

Danny exclaimed, "I've never seen a hotel suite this big before."

"Dis is bigger than my house." William added.

Auntie spotted the grand piano. "Oh, a piano!"

"Where do I sleep? Da sofa?" Asked William. Ruth went to another door and opened it. "William, this is your room."

"I get my own room?"

"This is the presidential suite. We each have our own room."

* * *

The sunlight streamed through the trees on the *Tavern on the Green* patio dining area where Ruth wearing a muumuu and Jim, Ruth's former television station owner, sat eating lunch.

"Ruth, the Emmy's are this evening. No matter what the outcome is, I would like to offer you a contract."

"Jim, I don't want to accept your contract. Danny and I have a perfect one with Al."

"The one I am offering you is better."

"Jim, how do you know what I have with Al?"

"It's better. Trust me. The contract is for a show that is much greater than *From the Big Apple* or *From da Big Island* ever could be." Jim retorted as he took a sip from his Manhattan. "It's an international travelogue show. I think you'll like the idea. You would go to different places throughout the country and the world showing us the out of the way places. It's never been done before."

"It's an interesting idea, and I like my semiretired life in Hawaii."

"You like New York, too, don't you?"

Ruth gave a slight but noticeable nod.

"And you like Hawaii, don't you?"

"Of course I do, Jim."

"It's the best of both worlds, Ruth. You can still live in Hawaii, come here and do the show."

"The eleven hour flights are too much for me, Jim."

"Eleven hours isn't that bad when you're traveling first class."

"I lose a day each way! Perhaps most of all, all those new post 9/11 restrictions are taking the fun out of air travel. Like air travel was ever fun." Ruth quipped as they both laughed.

"It's an opportunity for you to reinvent yourself and make more money. Think about it, Ruth."

* * *

Auntie and William, both in Aloha wear and zoris, strolled through Central Park walking by a pond loaded with ducks.

"William, you remember da duck pond in *Catcher in the Rye*?" William nodded as Auntie continued. "Dis is da duck pond."

"Der plenty of duck here." William retorted.

"What dat?" William asked as he pointed towards a couple of small animals that he had never seen before, they

117

looked somewhat like a mongoose, but were darker, had bushy tails, and climbed trees.

"Dey squirrel, dey all over da mainland."

Auntie and William continued their stroll through Central Park absorbing the scenery around them, the ducks, the squirrels, trees, and people strolling. As they approached the *Alice in Wonderland* statue they heard the all too familiar sounds of a ukulele strumming to an old Hawaiian song. There was a small crowd around a Hawaiian man wearing an Aloha shirt and Rayban sunglasses. As Auntie and William approached the man, they recognized Michael, Ben's brother. Upon seeing Auntie and William, Michael stopped singing and strumming, "Auntie! William! Aaa-loooo-haa!"

"Aaa-loooo-haa!" they reply.

The crowd realized the music would not begin for a while and dropped a few coins and dollar bills into the ukulele case and continued with their stroll through Central Park.

"What you do here?" Michael exclaimed.

"We here to see you, Michael." Auntie answered.

"You come all the way from da Big Island to see me?"

"Yups. We miss you. Ben and I need kokua. It time you come back to da island."

"I do oh-kay here. I make plenny money." Michael tried to convince Auntie who quickly realized he wasn't telling the truth.

"You make plenny money wid me on da island. You be mo happy."

"Ben misses you and we need you in Hawaii." William added.

"Come back wid us." Auntie urged.

"Please." William pleaded.

* * *

That evening, the door to the Presidential Suite swung open by Danny holding an Emmy in one hand, the door in the other. Ruth entered carrying an Emmy. She was followed by Linda and Pauline, her sister and niece. Behind them followed Auntie and William, all wearing formalwear. Danny closed the door behind him. The group moved into the suite sitting on the sofa and in the chairs surrounding the coffee table.

"We knew you would win." Pauline exclaimed.

"Yeah, *From da Big Island* is da bomb." William added.

Ruth placed her Emmy on the coffee table. Danny placed his next to hers.

"Don't they look great together?" exclaimed Danny. "I never knew they were this heavy."

"That reminds me of the first time I won. I almost dropped it on the stage."

"Aunt Ruth, Mother and I remember our going to Sardi's after the ceremony." Pauline reminisced. "Are we going this evening?"

Linda added, "Darling, Sardi's is a great place to celebrate."

"It never entered my mind to celebrate at Sardi's." Ruth responded.

Linda and Pauline both made pouting faces. Linda attempted to convince Ruth, "Darling, you've been away too long. We always celebrated at Sardi's. Don't you miss it here, Darling?"

"I used to, but not anymore."

"Darling, Pauline said Jim was going to make you an offer. Did he?" Asked Linda.

"Yes, Linda, he did."

"Why don't you take it and move back here? You can stay with us until you find a place."

Pauline perked up. "Oh, Aunt Ruth, that would be simply fabulous. Did Jim tell you I'd be the producer of your show?"

"We discussed it."

119

William looked concerned, "Are you thinking of leaving us?"

"Oh, Luka, you can't." Exclaimed Auntie, "Think about us. Da island."

"What would dat do to *From da Big Island*?" Danny asked.

"I never said I accepted Jim's offer. Jim made an offer. I turned it down."

Linda was always against her younger sister moving to the Big Island, thinking it was foolish and Ruth's way to escape Zach's untimely death. Linda couldn't take it anymore blurting, "Ruth, I've told you many times, Hawaii is no better than a third world country."

"It not bad!" Auntie proclaimed defending Linda's attack on Hawaii.

"Darling, the people are ill-educated."

"I'm almost educated." William added, "I graduate next month."

"Darling, All night, all I've been hearing is fragmented talk." Linda looked at Auntie, Danny, and William. "It's hard to understand you."

"It come wit time." Retorted Auntie.

Linda looked at Ruth, "Darling, you see what I mean? And you are willing to put up with it?" Ruth nodded. "Come back here to civilized New York."

"I'm civilized." William exclaimed.

"Hawaii civilized." Auntie added.

"Darling, you call *that* language civilized?" Linda asked Auntie.

"What you say, sista?" Auntie quipped.

"Darling," Linda addressing Ruth, "that's my point exactly. Come back here. Listen to that deplorable language."

"What wrong wit pidgin?" inquired Auntie.

"Darling, it is low class, like you." Linda snapped.

"I no low class."

Linda directed her attack towards Auntie, "Darling, listen how you speak. No one with a real education speaks like that."

"Wat you mean, sista?"

"Darling," Linda addressing Auntie, "you need to come to the United States and get a real education."

Ruth was becoming agitated with the way her elder sister was treating her Hawaiian ohana, especially Linda's latest United States statement.

"Linda, Hawaii *is* a state!" Ruth reminded Linda. "How do you know where Auntie was educated?"

"You go, sista!" Auntie encouraged Ruth.

Linda was looking a little confused, directed her next question to Ruth, "Darling, what's going on?"

"I'll tell you what's going on, *darling*." Ruth responded emphasizing the word darling. "Auntie speaks pidgin because she wants to speak that way, *darling*. She enjoys it, *darling*, and most of all it's expected, *darling*. You can stop using that damn *darling* shit because you cannot remember people's names. This is Auntie, this is William, and he is Danny." All three smiled and gave Linda a howdy wave.

"Ruth, darling," Linda retorted, "you surround yourself with people like them. What kind of life is that?"

"It's the kind of life I need and want. I enjoy my life on da Big Island. I chose to live there, not because I have to, but because, I like it there. I didn't know how much I liked it until this trip. New York no longer does it for me, all the rushing around and superficial people." Ruth pointed towards Auntie, William, and Danny continuing. "These people are my new family; the Hawaiians call it ohana. To put it more succinctly, I have more friends on da Big Island than I ever had here in the Big Apple!"

Ruth looked at Auntie, William, and Danny then at Linda and Pauline. "We have a long flight tomorrow. I don't want to go to Sardi's. It's late and we need to rest before our long flight." Ruth stood. "Now, Linda and Pauline, let's call it an evening."

Linda got up followed by Pauline. As they approached the door Pauline asked, "Aunt Ruth, what about the show?"

"I am not going to do the show. Jim will find someone else. Pauline, you will still be the producer."

Pauline ran over and hugged Ruth. "I love you, Aunt Ruth."

DA BATTLE

Back on the Big Island, Ruth was comfortably sleeping without the silk night mask. The sounds of grunting and popping were so loud it awakened her. She sat on the edge of the bed and slipped on her zoris, reached into her night stand, took out her flashlight, before going to the closet and took out the rifle.

Using her flashlight to guide her, Ruth made her way through the orchard towards the grunting and scratching sounds. The flashlight illuminated a large wild boar scratching the ground under a macadamia tree, with the flashlight in one hand and the rifle in the other hand, she rose the rifle feebly took aim and fired. The recoil of the rifle caused Ruth to drop the flashlight. When it landed, it fully illuminated the pig who looked at her, grunted then turned its attention to eat more fallen nuts.

A few moments later, in the distance, from the direction of Auntie's house, Ruth saw a figure with sole flashlight approaching her. It was Auntie also carrying a flashlight and rifle. As Auntie approached she yelled, "Luka, what da heck are you doing?"

"I'm going to get that damned pig!"

Auntie saw Ruth's flashlight illuminating the pig and directed her flashlight in the same direction as she approached Ruth.

"Thank, God! I thought it was da local boys trying to steal my keiki's."

Ruth and Auntie laughed as the pig started to trot towards Auntie's.

"Oh, no!" Auntie exclaimed, "I don't want him to get into da keiki's, he'll go lolo."

Using the light from Auntie's flashlight which was following the pig, Ruth could more accurately aim the rifle towards the pig. Carefully, she pulled the trigger.

* * *

Ruth, Auntie, and Ben were seated in lounge chairs on Auntie's lanai, each sipping red punch enjoying brownies.

"We tell no one that Luka kill pig." Stated Auntie.

"Luka, you in plenny trouble." Ben added.

"Trouble?"

"We next to state park. You must kill pig with bow and arrow. We need to get rid of da evidence."

"What evidence?" Ruth inquired.

"Da pig!" Auntie and Ben exclaimed.

After a moment, Auntie smiled and proclaimed, "We have luau!"

DA GRADUATION

A large green and white *Congratulations* *Graduates* sign
hung from the Honoka'a Gymnasium rafters. The
bleachers were filled with family members, among them
seated together, were Ruth, Ben, Auntie, Danny, Nalani
and Meka. Mickey and another cameraman, both wore
black *From da Big Island* T-shirts, were filming the
graduation.

On the court facing the bleachers were forty empty
seats and a podium. Michael, Ben's brother, holds his
ukulele off to one side maintaining a close watch behind
the bleachers. He got the signal and started strumming
and singing Queen Liliuokalani's *Aloha Oe*. Every one
stood as the students dressed in green graduation regalia
and gold tassels hanging from their green mortarboard
graduation caps walked from behind the stands to the
seating area. William was amongst the proud students who
waved at their families and friends.

* * *

The school's valedictorian had finished her speech and was returning to her seat from the podium. Mrs. Strong, wearing a green and white muumuu, returned to the podium and announced, "And now for our most improved graduate, William Ayala. Please approach the podium." The audience clapped as William proudly rose and walked to the podium. "Not only is he the most improved student," Mrs. Strong continued, "he is the first member of his family to graduate from high school." The crowd clapped and whistled as he made his way to the podium.

When William approached the podium, Mrs. Strong extended her right hand. William shook it. In her left hand was a plaque. The *From da Big Island* video crew was capturing the entire event as the high school and news photographers snapped Mrs. Strong presenting the award to William. Mrs. Strong moved back to the podium. "William, would you like to say a few words?"

"Yes, Mrs. Strong." William faced the crowd, specifically addressing his parents and Ruth in the stands. "I want to thank my mother and father. They had to put up with a lot from me." There was laughter throughout the crowd. "But, most of all I want to thank you Mrs. Strong, Dr. Tilton, Auntie, and Mrs. Newcomb for helping me get here." William winked at Ruth and Auntie. "Mahalo."

William started to turn to leave the podium, but quickly returned. "Oh, I almost forgot. Da pig for tonight's luau is from Mrs. Newcomb. Ma-ha-lo."

* * *

Later that evening, Mickey and the *From da Big Island* video crew were shooting the graduation luau festivities in Honoka'a Park; picnic tables filled with graduates, ohana, and friends. Tiki torches illuminated the *Congratulations*

Graduates sign which hung between two palms. Michael was among a group of performers who provided Hawaiian music for the graduation celebration.

Folding tables were filled with all the trimmings of a luau; one had chicken, the partially eaten pig, hamburger buns, and an assortment of utensils to cut and pull the pork off the pig. Another table had poi, brownies and other deserts, plates, glasses, and large five gallon jugs filled with red punch.

One picnic table had William, his parents, Nalani, and Meka on one side, the other his ohana and friends, Ruth, Auntie, Ben, and Danny all were enjoying the pig and all the trimmings.

"Ben, I still don't understand where da pig come from." Meka probed.

"Meka, I told you da pig kill Luka's cat. I use crossbow and kill da pig." Ben responded.

"You never use crossbow for pig before."

Ruth interjected, "There is always a first time for anything, isn't there?" She then used her spoon to eat what looked like purple pudding. This was the first time Ruth had poi. Upon tasting it, she grimaced. "This pudding is funny tasking. What is this purple stuff?"

"It poi." Nalani answered, "No use spoooon! Use fingers. Like this." She took her fore and middle fingers bringing them together, and showed Ruth how to scoop up and suck the poi off her fingers.

"It called, two finger poi!" Added William.

At that moment, Mickey arrived at the table motioning to Danny that he was set up for the closing. Danny looked at Ruth, "Luka, they are ready for you to shoot da closing."

Ruth looked at Mickey, "Bring the camera over here. I want to shoot my poi lesson before we do da closing."

"Luka, I'm already set up for da closing. Can we shoot that first, then shoot the poi sequence?" Mickey retorted.

"That will work for me."

Ruth and Danny got up heading to where Mickey had set up the camera. He handed Ruth a wireless lavaliere microphone which she put on her muumuu. As she did, she tells Mickey and Danny, "I don't want to do a run through. Let's shoot it."

Mickey had the camera pointed at Ruth who was standing looking into the camera. Mickey gave Ruth the signal to start.

Ruth smiled, "We learned a lot in this episode, including how to eat poi. I would like to dedicate this episode to William Ayala. I know he has a great future ahead of him. Until next time. This is Luka Newcomb, *From da Big Island.* Aaa-loooo-haa!"

EPILOGUE

In the years that followed my high school graduation, Luka, Auntie, and the Baccio's provided for my college education in English Literature here on the islands and then my journalism masters at USC in California. Between my studies, I was always able to find time to surf and documented my adventures in my surfing blog which *Surfer* magazine liked and later contracted me to write surfing articles. I posted short surfing videos on YouTube. Luka loved my videos and made arrangements to have me do a few surfing segments for *From da Big Island*. This not only gave me public speaking confidence and on camera experience, it opened doors for me. The surfing videos quickly morphed into *Da Wave with William* television show produced by Pauline, Luka's niece. I still travel around the world doing the things I love. None of this could of happened without the help of my ohana, Luka, Auntie, Charlene Strong, Dr. Tilton, and my folks.

Due to the escalation of the pig issue, following my high school graduation, Ben and Michael built fences around Luka's, Auntie's, and my folk's property. Sometimes, when a sounder of pigs breach one of our fences, Ben will dispatch them and fix the damage. Ben continues to help Luka and Auntie. Michael, in addition to helping Ben with his projects, has a regular gig playing at luaus and hukilaus, glad to have returned to the Big Island.

Joe and Eileen Baccio return to the Big Island a few times a year, primarily during the winter months, stay for a month or two at their Waikoloa Beach vacation home. Unlike Michael Corleone of *The Godfather* fame, Joe was able to get out of the mob, go legit, and became a proponent for the legalizing medicinal marijuana.

Auntie's medicinal marijuana research continued as she developed hybrid cannabis strains which increased the potency that better helped patients deal with pain without the psychotropic effects associated with marijuana. Many states have now legalized medicinal marijuana, while others have legalized its recreational use.

The call of the island was also felt by Gloria La Fong, who returned regularly over the years before retiring in Kona.

Luka was happy with her decision years ago to move out of her comfort zone and do something she had never done before; having the courage to take that chance and not be afraid of the unknown and made her move to the Big Island of Hawaii.

Luka eventually fully retired from show business, enjoying her retirement at Hale Newcomb. Once a month, she had *Girl's Day Out* when Luka, Auntie, Gloria, and Charlene would get together and have lunch at a old favorite or new restaurant, discussing books they had read, update each other on what was going on.

Luka became a well-known figure at the local libraries on the islands, with her *Reading with Luka* program where she would read a chapter from a book or have a visiting author read, but most of all encouraged everyone to read. She always ended her reading program much like she did her television shows, "Reading is an adventure. Until next time. This is Luka Newcomb, Aaa-loooo-haa!"

Glossary

The words below are utilized within this book and are intended to provide a basic reference. As with translations of any language, these words may have a more complex or multiple meanings. Not all pidgin words will be listed especially when the English word can be readily recognizable, such as da for the, den for then, dey for they, dis for this, and the like.

Aloha shirt: A man's Hawaiian shirt
Aloha: Hello or farewell
CEO: Chief Executive Officer
Da Boss: God
Da Bomb: The best
Gut: Good
Hale: House
Haole: White people or tourist
Hukilau: A beach celebration involving catching and cooking fish and other foods with live music and dance
Hula: Hawaiian dance
Imu: Hawaiian underground oven
Kahuna: An expert in a field or a Wiseman
Kam: Come
Kama'aina: A local person
Keiki: Child or little one
Kiawe: Mesquite tree
Klinim: Clean
Kokua: Help
Laikem: Like them
Lanai: Porch or veranda
Lei: A necklace of Hawaiian flowers
Lolo: Crazy or Loko
Luau: A large outdoor party with live music and dance generally with pig cooked in an Imu
Luka: Ruth in Hawaiian

Mahalo: Thank you

Mauka: Mountain or uphill side

Missionary dress: A long loose fitting dress with long sleeves and a high neck

Mo betta: More better

Mongoose: A long slender mammal that looks somewhat like a squirrel with short legs and a faintly bushy tail

Muumuu: Cut-off also a Missionary dress with short or no sleeves and an exposed neck

Nau: Now

Néné: Hawaiian geese

Nidim: Need them

Nui: Great, big, grand, much

Ohana: Extended Hawaiian Family

Pakalolo: Marijuana

Paniolo: Cowboy

Plenny: Plenty

Poi: A purple edible paste made from mashed fermented taro root

Shi shi: Urinate or use the bathroom

Slippahs: Slippers, zoris, flip-flops, sandals, or other slip-on footwear

To da max: To go all out

Ukulele: A small four stringed Hawaii guitar

Wikiwiki: Super-fast

Wok: Work

Zoris: Flip-flops, slippahs, go-aheads